THE
DOPEMAN'S
fine ass son's brothers

NASTEE

contents

Acknowledgments   v
Note to the readers   vii

Chapter 1   1
Chapter 2   8
Chapter 3   14
Chapter 4   21
Chapter 5   39
Chapter 6   45
Chapter 7   53
Chapter 8   59
Chapter 9   64
Chapter 10   69
Chapter 11   76
Chapter 12   85
Chapter 13   91
Chapter 14   107
Chapter 15   112
Chapter 16   129
Chapter 17   139
Chapter 18   143
Chapter 19   148
Chapter 20   159
Chapter 21   173
Chapter 22   182
Chapter 23   186
Chapter 24   191
Chapter 25   202
Chapter 26   208
Chapter 27   213
Chapter 28   219
Chapter 29   222

Chapter 30   225
Chapter 31   234
Chapter 32   239
Chapter 33   243

Cocaine   253
Lexxy   255
Quentin   257
Paul   259
Dutch   261
Wild Bill   263
Carley   265
Cocaine & Lexxy wedding   267
Make It Nastee   269
Acknowledgments   271

Stormeisha (Black Girl Tired BookTok)
Jazzy (The BookTok Rookie)
Shaunee (AudreyShanice)
Bewticious (B. Bewtie)
Shanny (BIH_IREADBOOKS)
Dosey-Dose (DoseofQ)
Lil' Baby AKA Jack-Jack (Resourcefulbooks)
Tash AKA Twinny (Tashtheauthor)
Arie My Personal Thelma
Joshua Matthews (Our only Tiktok Brother, lol)

The ENTIRE Boozy Book Baddies Community
BookTok
My Facebook Group: The Reading Chamber
Bookstagrammers
To everyone who read book 1, left a review, made a video… I LOVE YOUUUUU.

Remember I said before, in book ONE, this book will be predictable to some, and IS! I'm not here to give you shockable reads, but entertaining and RELATEABLE READS. THIS BOOK IS WRITTEN IN THIRD PERSON for a LARGER, BROADER outlook. I'm a storyteller… that's all I'ma do. Remember, this is a re-release, so if you read this previously on the Vampire Diaries, please just smile and share it with other people, lol. Mentionable Triggers: PROBABLY ALL OF THEM. Listen y'all, I can't be keeping up with everything in this book that might set someone aflame, lol. But… yes, Lucky is still alive, and so tf is Dutch, lol. Happy Reading <3

Also, there's a part of the last chapter that was used as the cliffhanger that you will see pop back up in book 3. <3

Also the images at the end are just interpretations… not too much.

The .22 caliber gun fell from Dutch's hand as the shocking news of Lexxy's parentage filled his ears. His hands flew up to his chest. It felt like a heart attack, but he was simply having his heart broken for the first time ever. He didn't understand how this could have happened.

Dutch's mind immediately went back to when he met Junie. Was it because of Wild Bill? Did he really want to know the truth? Had everyone he'd ever known and loved betray him?

Karma was a nasty bitch, but we all know Dutch deserved it the most. He was a monster in his own right, and he wasn't the only one who had been keeping secrets. The type of secrets that would ruin a family, a life, a dynasty.

"How? Junie, tell me how!" Dutch's voice boomed across the lawn, almost clearing out the wildlife that was nearby.

The birds flew across the sky in a hoard—something bad was definitely afoot.

"We don't have time for this right now, Dutch. We have to get to the hospital. Lexxy just collapsed."

If they weren't going to follow her out of the house, she didn't care. All she could think about was Lexxy, and if this time would be the last time she got to hold her daughter, to talk to her only child, to let her know for sure that she loved her. If this truly was it for her baby girl. No matter who the biological father was, that shit didn't matter in that moment, except for the fact that Wild Bill could be the key to saving Lexxy's life.

Regardless, Dutch dropping the gun gave Wild Bill the chance he needed to get away with his life. If he was being honest with himself, though he was pissed beyond belief, he didn't know if he actually had what it took to knock off his oldest friend in the world. Unfortunately, this would be the first and only time ever that he clenched or thought before he reacted.

As Wild Bill scuttled away, he ran after Junie to join her in the car. He had questions that needed answers as well. He just hoped that when he did ask, she would answer them and not beat around the bush. It wouldn't be a good time for her to lie either, because as much as he loved Junie, he would kill her dead for her betrayal, and then to tell a lie on top of that? Oh no, that would be more than he could take.

Dutch, noticing everyone was leaving, got up and headed for the inside of the house.

Poor Trisha laid in the backyard, bleeding from a leg wound, but she completed the mission that the boys couldn't—she got the golden bricks. Now, she just had to hope she didn't die behind all of this foolishness. The drama with Wild Bill being Lexxy's dad might have just saved her life. Sure, Dutch didn't want to lose a good soldier, but he didn't really give a fuck. There were more like her somewhere; losing one didn't change that. She was dispensable, at least in Dutch's mind she was.

Thankfully, Trisha had her phone in her back pocket, and she was able to roll herself on her side and make a phone call to one of the gorillas to come and pick her up. She wasn't going to the hospital though; she hated them. No, instead, she was going to thug it out, wrap that shit up herself, and keep it moving. As long as the bullet didn't get stuck inside her wound and she didn't bleed too much, she would be just fine.

Though the hospital doors were automatic, it was as if the anger, fear, and downright black power that flew off of Dutch, Wild Bill, and Junie forced the doors to open.

Junie's hair flew in the wind as she whipped around to the nurse's station. She asked where her daughter was, and the nurse could tell from the look on Junie's face and the way her voice shook, that it was dire, that the situation was clearly stressing her out, and the two men who stood behind her looked murderous, and she didn't want a scene in the waiting room because she'd already seen too much of that today.

She quickly typed in the information and pulled up her records.

"She's in the ICU right now. I'm sorry, ma'am, that's all the information I have for you, but if you want to go up to the fourth floor waiting room, where the actual ICU is, you may have better luck up there. Her doctor is Doctor Graham."

Junie was very happy to hear that the doctor who she'd been seeing was the doctor she was with now. He was very familiar with the case, so she had faith that her little girl would come out of this alright.

An hour passed before Doctor Graham came out with any news. The entire time, Cocaine just kept thinking about how things were getting much worse. He didn't even care about the gold at this point; he just wanted his woman to be ok, and he didn't know if that was going to happen. So much had transpired, and they still didn't even know the reason for Lexxy's collapse, but they were about to find out.

Doctor Graham came out with his clip board and a worried look on his face.

"Mr. Blackwood, Junie, Dutch, Bill," Doctor Graham greeted them.

They all said their respective hellos and waited to hear what Doctor Graham had to say.

"Unfortunately, Lexxy's other kidney, as we knew would happen, is failing her. Without a strong second one, she could possibly die. However, we've started her on dialysis, so hopefully that will stabilize her for now. She isn't in any pain, and I don't believe she suffered any pain during the collapse either."

They all heard what the doctor said, and Wild Bill was the only one who could provide a solution. He wished he would've known before now that he was Lexxy's father. Regardless of whatever problems he thought he had health wise, if he had a healthy organ to give her, he would.

Wild Bill stepped up from behind Junie, and he laid it all out on the table.

"Check this out, Doc, how long does Lexxy have before this one gives out? I just found out I'm her father, and if I can donate, I will. What do I need to do?"

Doctor Graham looked at him suspiciously. This was something that should have been said previously. Though it wasn't uncommon for most family members to not be good matches in the event of an organ transplant, but this right here, this was a mess.

Cocaine looked up with shock and horror in his eyes. He knew if there was any truth to this, there was definitely going to be hell to pay. Dutch wouldn't let this go so easily, especially not after Wild Bill switched up on him and helped to betray him, but it had to be like that. The shit had to be done. Dutch had it coming, but this, this was something that not even Cocaine could have foreseen.

"Typically, it takes a week to get those kind of results to see if you're a good match, but I can run the basic tests on you and see if we can come up with something a little faster. I'm going to need you to start filling out the paperwork. Jo Anne, can you get this man the proper paperwork for him to start filling out?" Doctor Graham spoke to his head nurse.

Doctor Graham had grown close to Lexxy in the time she'd spent at the hospital, and he hated to lose a patient. He just hoped that this would be what Lexxy needed.

Jo Anne walked away and came back with all the paperwork and told Wild Bill to follow her to the back so they could start the process. Though the dialysis would help for now, there was no telling how long it would last or if it would help at all. The fact was that Lexxy needed a kidney, and she needed one now.

Before Wild Bill went through the double doors for testing, he looked back at Junie and said, "On my life, if I can save our daughter, I will. I'll do everything I can to make sure she's OK."

Junie nodded her head, and she took a seat. This was just way too much for one day. Meanwhile, Dutch looked like he was going to lay Wild Bill out. He had so many emotions running through his body. It was as if his blood was boiling hot, and he wouldn't be surprised if he didn't pass out himself. How could this be? This was all a bit much, but one thing was for sure—Wild Bill was going to get his if Dutch had anything to do with it, and he would. He would make sure he paid for the stress and agony that this day had caused.

He kept looking over at Cocaine, who in this moment seemed calm and cool, but he was secretly plotting on what he would need to do to get Dutch out of the way.

Sure, he raised Lexxy, but he wasn't her father, and now, all the guilt and sorrow he felt for trying to take him out was gone. He didn't give a fuck anymore. He wanted that nigga's head, and he would have it on a silver platter with his eyes plucked out of his head. Yeah, that would be a sight to see....

Junie sat beside Cocaine, holding his hand, praying that things would work out. Cocaine had told Junie to go home and get some rest, but she kept refusing to leave Lexxy. There was no way she was going to leave her baby until she knew everything was OK, or at least that's what she thought.

The next day came and went, and they'd all been sitting at the hospital in the same clothes, looking dirty and stinking. They weren't allowed to see Lexxy just yet because she was getting rest, and Doctor Graham thought with all of the tension built up that when they did see her, it needed to be with good news, so he wanted them to wait to see if Wild Bill was a match.

Junie was tired, and she kept nodding off, but the memory of her and Bill's relationship kept flashing back through her mind like an old movie. She thought of how madly in love she was with him at one point in time and how happy they were together. This was something she often thought about when she rested her head, or when she was traveling. That was the life she and Wild Bill were supposed to have together, but the cards they had been dealt were laid out differently, and they weren't going to be able to have that life...

"Bill, I love you, but something has got to change. You gotta get out them streets."

"Ju-Ju, I need you to keep it cool. I got one more thing to do, well, a couple of other things to do, and then we'll be straight. We won't have any more problems, and everything will be just fine," Wild Bill said as he whispered in Junie's ear. They were lying in the bed of their two-story home. It was cute, but very small, but Junie didn't care about the money. All she cared about was Bill and their happiness, and overall, their safety, but Junie had been hatching a plan. She didn't want Bill to go to jail for selling drugs. She didn't want him to go to jail at all, and with all the time she'd seen the people she knew getting because of it, she was ready for Bill to let it go.

Junie had met Dutch a year or so before when he tried talking to her. He was instantly taken by her, but she loved Bill, and though she thought Dutch was cool, a smooth talker, and somewhat handsome, she was crazy about her own man, and Junie wasn't a cheater, but she also knew what Dutch had, and if she could get Wild Bill in, down with his crew, she knew he'd have the protection and the resources to make money but still stay out the street.

Wild Bill was strong, and he was an amazing fighter. Junie heard through the grapevine that Dutch's soldiers kept getting killed off because they weren't skilled, and they were stupid. They didn't take orders well, and they didn't know how to do anything but slang dope, but Wild Bill was different. He was smart, strategic, and his hands were lethal. There were so many people who were afraid of Wild Bill from his beatdowns alone, so when Junie heard that Dutch could use a helping hand, she didn't hesitate to try to help him, while helping Wild Bill at the same time.

Junie waited until Wild Bill had passed out from their long but very intimate love making session and crawled out of the bed to go downstairs and use her phone. She knew how to get in contact with Dutch, and she had been speaking to him little by little to get him to trust her. Dutch didn't know that Wild Bill and Junie were a couple. She'd made it seem like Wild Bill was just a trusted friend, or even a brother of some sort. Dutch was so naïve then, and he didn't think twice about it whenever Junie mentioned him. Well, it could've been naivety or just arrogance, either way, it didn't matter. Junie was trying to help her man.

"Hello?" Junie said into the phone, using her seductive yet cool voice.

"Hey, beautiful. How ya' doin'?" Dutch asked, excited to hear from Junie. She only called twice a week. She wasn't clingy, and she had a killer body. That alone was enough to make Dutch pay attention to her.

"I'm OK, how are you?"

"Shit, I'd be better if you were lying in my bed at night, letting me hold you and spoil you. What you got goin' on?"

Junie rolled her eyes. She knew what Dutch wanted with her was more than just sex. He wanted a full-blown relationship with her, but she didn't want that, not with him. It wasn't that she didn't like Dutch; had she been a single woman, she probably would've been thrilled that he was trying to court her, but she didn't want him. She never wanted to be a drug or crime lord's wife. She wanted to be with Wild Bill forever, but she knew what that came with, and she didn't think she'd be willing to do that for anyone else but him.

"Well, I called because…I kind of need a favor."

"OK, anything, baby. Shoot!"

Junie took a deep breath, making sure she worded her sentences properly.

"I heard through the grapevine you need security or something of the sort. Is that right?"

Dutch laughed into the phone. "Yeah, how you hear that?" he asked curiously.

"The streets talk, and even when I'm not trying to listen, I still hear things, but I might be able to help you out."

"Yo, if you tell me you a cold-hearted killer, I ain't gon' be no more good, baby."

"No, no, not me. You remember I told you about Wild Bill, right? Well, he's a good dude. He's trying to get out of actually selling drugs, so I figured maybe you could help put him on."

"Mmm…and if I do this for you, what will you do for me?"

The truth was, Junie didn't want to have to do anything. She didn't want anything to do with Dutch, but if this was the only way, then she'd make it happen. She'd make it possible.

"Well, I guess whatever I can do. I can do secretarial work if you have any of that floating around."

Junie had gone to college to be an administrative assistant, but after a few years of that, she realized she wanted to help others find assistants, but she didn't have the money for her own start-up business, so for now, that was just a dream.

"Nah, I don't need none of that. I ain't makin' calls and shit. I need you, a queen by my side. Somebody when I come home, I can come home to them. Somebody who ain't gon' milk me dry. I'm surrounded by bitches who want in, but they ain't down for the ride."

"And what makes you think I am?" she asked. Junie was a lot of things, but she didn't know if being a ride or die was truly one of them. Though she had held down the home front for Wild Bill whenever he did his stints in jail, she never considered herself the *real rider type. She was doing what she thought most women would do in that type of situation, but that was the old school for you.*

"I just can tell. Something about you is different, baby. I'd be a fool to let you slip through my fingers. We can take it as slow or as fast as you want. I don't wanna pressure you; I wanna win your heart fair and square. I wanna show you that it's a lot more to me than drugs and flashy shit. I am a gentleman, and a man first. I need love like everybody else."

Dutch had always been honest with her, and even though he was a smooth talker, he always gave her facts. He wasn't just talking for the sake of hearing his own voice. He truly did need a queen, a woman to call his own.

"Well, I suppose that would be alright. Do I need to get you in contact with Bill…or?"

"Nah, baby. I know how to find him, and I even know how to find you. I just ain't the stalker type, so I let you be, but here's what you can do, call me in a couple of days. Tell your boy, 'Wild Bill,' that I'll get up with him soon."

"Thank you so much, Dutch."

"No, thank you. You done made my whole night."

Junie smiled into the phone as if Dutch could see her, and then she ended the call and worked her way back upstairs.

"Junie, Junie!" Doctor Graham called, snapping her back into reality. She looked around and realized she was in the hospital. She was waiting on news about Bill and Lexxy.

"Yes, Doctor? I'm sorry, I was…I was someplace else."

Dutch came up beside them and grabbed Junie's hand. He hated all of them for what they had done, but he loved Lexxy, whether he was her father or not. He'd raised her, watched her take her first steps, heard her first words. She was his child regardless.

"Yes, well, I have good news. It seems as though Bill may be a good fit. I'm not sure how long it will work because he is a bit older, but despite all of his drinking and age, his kidneys seem to be in good health, and so is his body. I think we may be able to do the transplant. I'm still waiting on a few test results to come back, but so far, it's looking up."

Doctor Graham reached for Junie's hand, and he looked at Cocaine with a smile plastered across his face. This whole time, shit hadn't been working out, but maybe, just maybe this time, God was smiling on them and was going to let Lexxy live. Besides, there would be no story without her after all, right?

"So, you sure this is gonna work, Doc?" Wild Bill asked Doctor Graham who was standing over him, prepping him for emergency surgery. The faster they could get the kidney out of Wild Bill and into Lexxy, the better it would be.

Junie stood to the side of the bed, holding Wild Bill's hand, saying a prayer over him and remembering how things used to be between them; how they were madly in love and nothing could've come between them. She still was holding onto Wild Bill in her heart; in truth, she'd never really stopped loving him, and she wouldn't as long as she had breath in her body.

She leaned over the bed and kissed him on the cheek, and whispered a soft, "Thank you" in his ear before they pushed him to the back of the hospital. Junie would've never thought in a million years any of this would happen, but what happens in the dark, sometimes comes to light, and it isn't that secrets can't stay buried, because they can, but every now and then, when something needs to happen, it does. Finding out Wild Bill was Lexxy's father saved her life. Junie only asked that no one tell her about it being Wild Bill until everything with the surgery went ok. She didn't want that to be the way Lexxy found out.

Now that Wild Bill was being prepped for surgery and Junie had caught her breath, she had to deal with Dutch. He wasn't letting this issue go, not for one second, and she knew eventually, she'd have to face the monster that was her husband.

"So, they gon' take him back and she's gon' be ok, right?"

"Yeah, hopefully. If the surgery is a success, then she'll be just fine," Junie said in an exhausted voice. She was tired and overwhelmed.

"Good, good. Now, you know you got to tell me what the fuck happened, right? How is this nigga her father? Was you cheatin' on me, Junie? All these years, I thought you were the good one; that I was the only fuck up. But now, here we are, and the truth comes out, that you was just bein' a hoe."

Junie stepped back in shock. *Did he just call me a hoe?* She knew he was mad, but the name calling was uncalled for.

"First of all, I didn't cheat on you, so you need to just cool your fuckin' jets. If you give me a moment to explain, then I will."

"Please, be my muthafuckin' guest. It's the least you could do."

Junie went back into her mind to recollect the part of the story he didn't know, and she began explaining as best she could.

Wild Bill had been working for Dutch for a solid two years.

Everything was going well, and she was taking her time with Dutch. She wasn't leading him on, at least not to her she wasn't. She was building a strong friendship between the two, because at the end of the day, she had asked him for a favor, and she did have to hold up her end of the deal, and she was. Dutch promised her they could go slow, as slow as she wanted, and she was. She was going terribly slow.

Junie had told Wild Bill about the agreement she made with Dutch after a little while, just so he would know, and so he wouldn't accidentally ruin things for himself. He trusted Junie, so he knew she wasn't going to cheat on him, not in a real sense. Sure, she had to spend a little time with him here and there, she even had to go on a few dates, but she never kissed him and never gave him more affection than a hug, so that was fine; it was no big deal to him, not really. He was finally able to take care of her the way he said he would, so why would he give a damn? What was it for him to worry about…nothing…or so he thought.

Dutch wanted Junie all to himself; he always did, but he never knew he was competing with Wild Bill. He just always assumed Junie was very conservative, a good girl, so he did things her way, but he got Wild Bill out of the way without even knowing he changed all of their lives forever.

Dutch had an enemy so fierce, that no matter how he came at him, he couldn't win. He burned his trap houses down, the nigga bounced right back. He killed his family, and he only went harder, but with Wild Bill on Dutch's side, there was nothing he couldn't do.

The first time Wild Bill went to jail for conspiracy for murder, he was bonded out, and eventually, the charges were dropped. No witnesses, no case. The shit was dead. Wild Bill had done a lot of killing for Dutch, and he didn't mind. Most of the people he killed, it was for a good enough reason he felt like, plus, he was making more money than he'd ever seen. He was a real problem in the streets, but at home, he was a gentle teddy bear with Junie.

But, Wild Bill crossed the wrong man for Dutch, and it ended in a string of jail time. A few months here and there for possession of drugs, a few months for lying to the police, beating up the police, and eventually, a murder, and it had all become too much for Junie to take. She'd been there for him through it all, but the murder, not the actual act, but the time he was going to have to do behind it was too much for her to handle. Her heart was weak after finding out about how much time he was going to do. Luckily, they had the best lawyers in the city, so Wild Bill was able to stay home during the trial and wait, and that was when Lexxy was conceived, in a moment of sadness and pain, because she knew she was going to be losing Wild Bill for some time, they slept together one last time.

A week before Wild Bill went to prison, she found out she was pregnant, and she knew if Dutch found out that it was someone else's baby, or that there was even someone else, he wouldn't continue to foot the bill on Wild Bill's prison expenses, and so much more. She knew how possessive Dutch could be, and she didn't want the love she had for Wild Bill to endanger either one of their lives, so when Wild Bill went to prison, she didn't tell him right away about the baby. She waited a little time, but she was able to trick Dutch into believing that the only reason she was taking things slow with him was because she was afraid something would happen to him and she didn't want to be out in the world alone, fending for herself. Yeah, right. Wild Bill had trained Junie like he would a regular soldier. She could take care of herself if need be, but Dutch didn't know it then, and he still didn't know.

After Wild Bill went to prison, Junie began taking things with Dutch more seriously. At first, it was a ploy to keep her and Wild Bill alive and safe and taken care of, including her child, but then,

She of course never told Wild Bill about the baby being his, only that she was born, because she knew what would happen, and it was exactly what was about to happen. Wild Bill and Dutch would be in a fight over it, a fight that would pay with someone's life.

"So no, I didn't cheat on you. I lied, but I didn't cheat on you."

"You might as well have! How the fuck I know you and that nigga ain't have somethin' goin' on this whole time behind my fuckin' back?"

"All I can do is say we didn't! You see how shocked he was about finding out Lexxy was his daughter? You think he would be acting so shocked if we had something going on? Don't you think I would've told him by now if there was something? Come on now, Dutch. You're a lot of things, but stupid ain't one of 'em."

Dutch reacted before his brain could truly process what just happened.

He snatched Junie up by her throat and threw her up against the wall. There was no one there to see what was happening. The waiting room was empty, and the nurse had stepped away for a moment.

Cocaine was finally able to see Lexxy, well, more so like he snuck in to see her, so there was no one there to see what he was doing.

Junie struggled to breathe under Dutch's grip, and her brain felt like it would explode from all the pressure of her trying to catch her breath.

"After all these fucking years and all I've given you. I trusted you, Junie! I trusted you with my heart, my life, my world, and this is the type of shit you repay me with? Whether he was her father or not, I'm your husband, and you're supposed to be on my side always! I thought you were a real rider."

Junie's breath was literally being torn from her body, but in a weak attempt to save her life, she remembered the training Wild Bill had taught her all those years ago.

With everything in her, she kneed Dutch in the balls. She kicked him as hard as Thor's hammer hits.

"Agghh! You bitch!" he cried before toppling onto the ground.

"I ain't gon' be too many more bitches, you understand? The next time you call me out of my name or even look like you gon' put your hands on me, I'ma whoop your ass. You done lost your fuckin' mind, Dutch."

Junie didn't stop there though. As he lie on the ground, Junie kicked him, repeatedly. She was so angry, not even really with him, but with herself for the secret she kept that could ruin her family, not that they'd been much of a family the last year or so. Lexxy being shot, losing a kidney, Wild Bill being her father, so many things were happening over the course of such a small amount of time, and there just wasn't enough retribution. No time, no repayment, no relief.

The only thing that stopped Junie from kicking the

shit out of Dutch was Cocaine reappearing from Lexxy's room. At first, when he saw her, he thought his mind was playing a funny trick on him. He'd love to see Dutch in pain getting whooped on by anyone, but when he realized it was real, he didn't want to stop it, and it was that reason alone that Junie did stop. She was embarrassing her husband whether there was someone in the room or not, and the simple fact that Cocaine was the one to see him getting his ass beat, wasn't at all satisfying to her.

When she saw Cocaine's face, she immediately quit kicking him. She grabbed her purse, and out the door she went. She hadn't stomped anybody in a long time. Junie was about that life and from the projects of South Nashville. Dutch had her fucked up, and this was only the beginning of their marriage falling apart.

ocaine couldn't believe what he'd just witnessed. He knew Junie probably was about that life, but he didn't know it was to the point where she would fight Dutch. He needed a good ass kicking though, but the fact that Junie was the one to give it to him was what fucked Cocaine up the most, that and then finding out that Wild Bill was really Lexxy's father was world blowing. It was too much for it to just be mind blowing.

But he was just happy that Wild Bill would be able to fix Lexxy's kidney problem. Her passing out might have made her own life flash past her eyes, but it also made Cocaine's. Since it happened, he kept envisioning a life with Lexxy ripped away from him and ruined. The happiness he'd been hoping for since he met her was once again threatened. This shit had to stop. It wasn't fair. Lexxy was a good woman, and she lived a good life. She didn't deserve to have something like this happen to her. The only person he wished would get sick and die was Dutch, and since that probably wasn't going to happen, he had to let that dream go.

While Wild Bill was in the back, getting ready for his surgery, so was Lexxy. Cocaine wasn't completely sure of the process or how long it would take, but he knew he needed to go back in the room with her before she went to the back. He'd stepped out for a minute just to go get something to drink, but then he saw her mom and Dutch, and that threw his whole plan off, so he wasn't sure what was going on with that, but it was time for him to get back to his baby.

Cocaine went and got something to drink like he said he would, but he didn't want to drink it in front of Lexxy because she wasn't allowed to have anything to eat or drink for sixteen hours before her surgery, and she'd been complaining that she was thirsty. He'd be glad when all of this was over because he was tired of seeing his baby suffer.

He went to the vending machine and got a Sprite. There was something about the way the carbonation bubbled through his soul that was always exhilarating, plus, Coke was a dark drink, and that shit was bad for your liver, per the doctor's advice. He'd stopped drinking most dark liquids to try and encourage a healthy lifestyle for Lexxy.

Cocaine popped the top on his Sprite and guzzled most of it down while he was still at the vending machine. He knew Lexxy would smell it on his breath when he kissed her, so he felt bad, but she would just have to get over it. He was fucking thirsty, and if he could, he would have gone to the liquor store and got him a Corona. He could probably down a whole six-pack at this point. Cocaine wiped his mouth to free him of any liquids; Lexxy had a habit of licking his lips whenever he had juice or any liquid around his mouth, and she wasn't allowed to have any liquids whatsoever. He was afraid that the smallest breaking of any rule could put her at risk during her surgery, and after the last two days, really the last year, he didn't want anything else to happen.

When he stepped into the room, Lexxy was sitting up with a smile on her face.

"What you smilin' about?" Cocaine asked as a smile spread across his lips, matching Lexxy's.

"I don't know, I just have a good feeling. How are you feeling about this whole situation?"

"Shit, I never been happier, baby. This is finally your chance. You gon' be feelin' good, you always look good, and I'll finally be able to marry my baby, so shit, I'm ready for them to take you back there and slap that kidney inside of ya', and then I'm tryna put a baby inside of ya'."

Lexxy giggled. She couldn't believe he was talking like that at a time like this. She was preparing to go back into surgery, under the knife—a place she'd been too many times at this point. She never thought she'd ever have to surgery or anything serious for that matter, at least not until she had a baby, and now, she wasn't sure if that was possible. She didn't know if she'd be able to have kids because of how broken down her body was, but she still loved Cocaine, and she would do everything to see his legacy fulfilled, even if that meant having a baby that could potentially kill her during childbirth, or if she were fortunate enough to live, her body be out of shape and out of whack, but hey, it's a baby, right? The only hope for the future.

"So, did they say where the kidney came from?" Lexxy asked as she stared at the TV. Cocaine didn't want to lie to her, but he knew he damn sure couldn't tell her like this, but before he spoke, she asked another question.

"And where the hell is Denise? Why hasn't she been here? Is something wrong, and I don't know it?"

Cocaine didn't know the answer to that either. He'd been calling and calling, but she was nowhere to be found, so he'd wondered the same thing, but he didn't want to be in Denise's business, but now, since Lexxy was asking for her, he figured he might have to go looking for her. Besides, it was strange for Denise not to show up when being called and text a million times. Cocaine just hoped she wasn't up to anything shady; they had plenty of shady in their lives and didn't need anymore.

"Knock, knock! Can I come in?" a woman wearing a nurse's uniform with a blue hair cap and a white mask over her face entered the room.

"Of course, is it time?" Cocaine asked as he looked into Lexxy's eyes. He didn't see fear nor pain, but strength and love. Lexxy was one of the strongest people he had ever met, and that strength is what gave him the strength to carry on in these rough and uncertain times.

"Yes, sir. Lexxy, are you ready?"

"I am."

Cocaine grabbed Lexxy's face and smooshed his lips with hers. The kiss was sloppy and long, but he wanted to make sure in case something happened, if something went wrong, they'd both have that moment together.

"Ok, ok, you'll get her heart too worked up beforehand, and there are still a few things we need to do. Sir, do you mind stepping outside?"

"Not at all."

Cocaine was used to not being able to be in the room when they needed to do something with Lexxy, so this was normal to him.

He went outside and joined Junie, who had just come back from taking a breather outside, and who still looked like she was shaken up from what happened with Dutch, but not in a scared way; she just looked homicidal.

Denise sat on her couch, smoking a blunt, something she rarely ever did, but this was all a bit too much. Things were happening very quickly, and she needed to get herself together.

When Junie called Denise and told her what happened, she wanted to instantly jump up and head to the hospital, until she heard the conversation on the other end of the phone because in the moment, she wasn't thinking about hanging up; she completely forgot, but that didn't stop her from hearing the voices on the other end.

"See, now all of this mess is going on and my baby done collapsed. I don't care what y'all do after this, but don't tell Lexxy about this shit. She doesn't need to hear about Bill being her father until all of this is over with. Whatever is wrong with her, I don't won't this to fuck her up even more or put stress on her, period!"

Denise didn't want want to hang up the phone before now, but hearing that, she knew it was time. All of these years, she wasn't crazy, and that day she overheard Junie on the phone, she had indeed heard what she thought she did.

Denise and Lexxy were seventeen years old, and it wasn't strange or unlike Denise to show up at the house unannounced. All of the ground's people and servants knew who she was, and they loved her like they loved Lexxy, so when she came over, they treated her like she lived there and just let her do her own thing.

On this one particular day, Denise came over to surprise Lexxy. It was right before their high-school graduation, and Denise had gotten her this bracelet they'd seen at Tiffany's. She wanted to give it to her before they graduated so she could wear it with her outfit. When she got in the house, and it was a big house, she didn't see or hear anyone, so she was on her way up the stairs to Lexxy's bedroom. As she passed by the bathroom, she heard something that sounded like whispering, and she thought maybe it was Lexxy sneaking and talking on the phone, something she often did whenever she didn't want her parents to know she was talking to someone who wasn't considered "like them."

Denise put her head up to the door and listened to the conversation. Immediately, she recognized the voice to be Junie's, but it was what she heard as soon as she put her ear to the door that made it hard for her to pull away.

"Yes, Mama, I know. I can never tell Lexxy, and don't you tell her either. I'm only telling you now because I've been dreaming about it more and more, every night. It's starting to weigh heavily. Bill being her father, I just…I can't tell him, I can't tell her, I can't

tell anyone, but I know I can trust you. Mama, promise me you'll never tell, you'll never tell the truth about Wild Bill and Lexxy."

The bracelet fell from Denise's hands, but she quickly picked it up and sought refuge inside the hallway closet so Junie wouldn't see her. She waited until Junie came out of the bathroom and disappeared before she found her way to Lexxy's rom, and when she got inside, she acted as if everything was normal, although it wasn't. She would never forget that moment, and she'd been carrying it around for almost ten years now. She'd never told anyone, and she wished she would have because she didn't have anyone to share the secret with, but she knew how badly it would hurt Lexxy to know, no matter when she found out, and that was why she'd been keeping her distance. With everything falling apart, she saw something bad coming, and she didn't want to have to lie and pretend as if she didn't know, when in actuality, she did. Sure, nobody knew she knew, but she knew she did.

She would never want to upset Lexxy purposely or hurt her, but she thought, at least when she was younger that keeping this secret was helping her. She now felt guilty and partially responsible for Lexxy not being able to get a kidney sooner. If she would've just said something, maybe what she was going through now wouldn't be happening. How was she going to face her best friend now, knowing that she actually knew? She hated to lie, and she never had. This was the only thing that was a secret in their friendship, and deep down, she worried it would ruin what they had.

"So, are you nervous about the transplant?" the nurse, who seemed a bit too young to be a nurse, asked.

"Uhm…no, I don't think so. I'm honestly ready to just get it over with."

"I can only imagine so, but I guess it's too bad you won't be making it there."

From behind the nurse's back, she pulled out a large syringe from her the waistband of her pants, covered Lexxy's mouth with her other hand, and plunged it directly in her neck, making Lexxy instantly pass out.

Her job was done. She knew the medicine would only put her to sleep, but Lexxy was on dialysis and on oxygen, but all of that shit was about to get unplugged. The nurse unplugged every machine connected to Lexxy's body and smiled at her handy work. She had finally done it.

And the best part to her was, this wasn't even planned. She made something happen without even having to make too much of an effort, and she loved it. She was able to keep the machines from beeping because sometimes they still did even after being disconnected, and she walked out of her room, acting as if nothing had happened. Nobody ever thought to ask her name, or wonder why she wasn't appropriately dressed as a floor nurse. She snuck in dressed like she was ready to go into surgery, but Lexxy wasn't going to surgery for a few more hours. That just goes to show how negligent the hospital could be at time. Missing babies, nurses sneaking in rooms and shit; this facility was not secure, and once again, Lexxy's life was at stake.

As soon as the devious nurse exited Lexxy's room, she went and got on the elevator immediately. She wasn't even supposed to be coming in that day, but she came in for a few hours to check on some of her favorite patients, and when she saw Lexxy's name come across one of the nurse's boards, she realized it wasn't a coincidence; this was fate.

Though this woman, the nurse, seemed to be completely normal, she lived a secret life. Her brothers, Paul and Quentin, were the head of the Lischey Avenue gang, the second largest gang in Nashville, after the Gorilla gang.

Upon seeing Lexxy some time ago in the hospital, she didn't know she was. She didn't care anything about her until her brothers had come up with a plan that would help keep them in power. She wasn't supposed to have anything to do with it, and she had no idea when it was going to happen or where it was going to take place, but the simple fact that she was able to help made her feel good. Not to mention it was all her brothers talked about, day in and day out, and she was tired of hearing them go on about this woman. Her time had finally come for her to prove herself. Paul and Quentin constantly teased her because she became a nurse instead of going straight into the drug business like them, but it was their sister's nursing degree that had helped to save them many times. It was her nursing expertise that kept them alive, and believe it or not, in this instance, it had been something that helped do them a favor.

As she got on the elevator and the doors closed in front of her, she knew she had done an amazing thing, and she couldn't wait until they officially pronounced her dead.

"Shouldn't she have been taken down by now? Maybe we need to check in to see what the nurse said to her," Junie said as she looked at Cocaine worriedly. Wild Bill had been in the operating room for a long time, and she figured Lexxy would be going down at some point, a lot sooner than it was happening.

Cocaine nodded his head in agreement and got up to check on Lexxy. When he went in, he immediately knew something was wrong. The machines were dim, where the lights were usually brightly lit up, and Lexxy seemed to be sleeping which was strange because just twenty minutes or so before, she seemed to be wide awake.

Cocaine went to the side of her bed and shook her lightly. "Baby, baby?" he said as he continued shaking her.

But she was nonresponsive; she didn't move even a little bit.

"Lexxy? Baby, can you hear me?"

Cocaine looked over at her heart monitor, and nothing was happening. Her chest wasn't even rising and falling like it normally did.

Realizing something was wrong, Cocaine ran out to the nurse's station, yelling for someone to help Lexxy.

"Please, something is wrong with her! Help my baby, please."

The nurse ran into the room, picked up her wrist, and realized she had a pulse, but it was very faint. She got on the help phone and called for the doctor and other nurses to come in and help her.

The doctor ran in and noticed the cords were unplugged. He had a confused look on his face, but there wasn't time to ask questions. He had to get Lexxy hooked back up immediately and see if they could wake her up.

Doctor Graham pushed Cocaine to the side, really to the back, behind the nurses and plugged the machines up, calling for them to do what they could to save her life.

This was all happening too fast for Cocaine. Just when he thought things couldn't get any crazier, they had gotten even worse.

Cocaine stepped out of the room to inform Junie of what was going on, and she just couldn't take it. It was as if her heart was breaking all over again for her daughter, and now, with things going south, she wondered if she'd be able to still get the transplant, but they couldn't ask anyone. All they could do was wait patiently, hoping Lexxy was going to be alright.

A few hours later, Lexxy was stabilized, and she was ok. Doctor Graham ran several tests to make sure she was ok, and they found heavy doses of chloroform in her system, which was crazy because they obviously hadn't given her any, and it was dangerous for her to be around it.

Doctor Graham didn't have any explanation as to where it came from or what happened, and he had to be honest with Cocaine and Junie about the situation. Dutch had long ago gone home; the stress and truth of the day had overtaken his emotions, so the only person Junie had to rely on was Cocaine. Denise had been on her way for hours now, and Junie wasn't sure if she ever showed.

At this point, Junie knew she had to come clean about the Wild Bill situation. With the way things were going, she didn't know if her daughter was going to make it from one minute to the next, and she didn't want her to go out of this world not knowing the truth.

They put Lexxy's transplant on hold for the moment, but the family was told they could go in and spend time with her for a little while. Junie had called Dutch several times since Lexxy had been brought back to the land of the living, though she didn't completely flat line, she was damn near there, but Dutch wasn't answering. He wasn't picking up the phone, nor responding to the text messages she sent, and she didn't know what that was about, but she would figure it out later.

Before Junie and Cocaine went in to see Lexxy, Denise finally showed up, coming through the double doors of the hospital glowing, but her eyes were swollen and red. This shit was like déjà vu to all of them. It was never ending, and they spent more time at the hospital than anywhere else.

"Denise, so nice of you to show up," Junie said

sarcastically, wondering where she'd been this whole time.

"I'm sorry I'm late. I was just…just trying to get it together."

This was true. Denise was trying to get her life together because eventually, the truth was going to come out, and she was afraid of what would happen when it did, but she wasn't going to say that. Denise had been kept up to speed as to what was happening with her home girl, and now, she just wanted to be there for her.

The three went into the room with Lexxy, and she was sitting up in her bed drinking some juice. After having waited all day, she was thirsty, and since she wasn't going to be able to get the transplant now for a little while, she was able to eat and drink. She felt like a newborn baby being fed for the first time.

When the door opened and Denise walked in, she was so happy to see her. She felt like Denise had been being distant, and she didn't know what the cause of it was, but she hoped to find out soon.

"Denise!" Like a child, Lexxy reached her arms up waiting for a hug from her best friend. It didn't matter how badly she felt; she truly was happy to see her bestie come through the door.

"Hey, girl. I heard you up here giving everybody a scare. You good now, though?"

"I think so. The nurse I had before, well before whatever happened to me, they can't find her. I told them she came in here and was talking to me, and then boom, she stuck me with a syringe, but they have no camera footage on this floor, so it could have been anyone. I'm just hoping it wasn't anyone else from Dad's past; we can't take any more of that. Speaking of which, where's Unc and Daddy?" Lexxy asked peaking around them to see if maybe they were coming in afterwards.

Junie stepped up to the front, wedging her way in between Cocaine and Denise. Cocaine already knew what was about to go down, so she went near the window and began staring out of it. Denise was clueless. She hadn't been there, so she truly didn't know what was happening, thank God.

"Well, baby, I need to talk to you about that."

"Oh God, don't tell me something happened to one of them, please Mommy, I can't take it."

"No, no, nothing like that, but this will be very difficult for you to hear, but I'm hoping you see the light at the end of the tunnel when I finish telling you this story."

Lexxy held a perplexed look on her face. She couldn't imagine what her mother was about to tell her, but whatever it was, it must have been serious because tears filled her eyes, and several slid down without warning or her permission.

"What is it, Mommy?" Lexxy asked, grabbing ahold of her mother's hand.

"Oh, baby," Junie paused as she rubbed Lexxy's hand and then her forehead, and then she continued, "Dutch isn't here because he's mad, very, very mad. Dutch and Wild Bill were at the house, with Cocaine. They got into it about some buried treasure in the backyard, and Dutch was about to kill Wild Bill."

Lexxy gasped in shock and covered her mouth. She

felt like she was watching a soap opera because she could actually picture what her mother was saying.

"Then, when I came in to tell them we needed to get to the hospital, and I saw them, I couldn't let your father kill him."

"Well, of course not, we're family."

"Yeah, but not in the way you think…"

Cocaine turned around from the window and shook his head. There was no soft way to tell her or a way to sugarcoat it; she just had to put on her grown woman panties and spill the beans.

"What do you mean, not in the way I think?"

Lexxy's eyebrows raised, and a frown came across her face. She was interested in what her mother was trying to tell her.

"Well, sweetheart," Junie said through trembling lips. "Wild Bill….he-he's…Oh God, this is so hard."

"Just say it, Mother!"

"He's your father! Ok, there, I said it. Wild Bill is your father."

Cocaine came closer to the bed, expecting for Lexxy to pass out, or for her heart monitor to start beeping like crazy, but that didn't happen. Instead, Lexxy broke out into the loudest, strangest laugh. Her head even fell back she was laughing so hard.

"Lexxy, baby?" Cocaine asked as he grabbed her hand. "You ok?"

"Ha! I'd be a lot better if y'all quit playin' jokes on me. That shit ain't funny, Mommy. Now, what do you really wanna tell me? I believe the part about Daddy and

Unc gettin' into it, but Wild Bill being my daddy? You just need to stop."

"Lexxy, I'm not playing, baby. I'm not joking. Where do you think your transplant came from? Wild Bill is giving you your kidney, baby."

Lexxy's world had already spun out of control, but this shit was like the big bang was happening in her mind. How could this be? How could Wild Bill be her real father?

"Explain, now!" Lexxy was ready to go the fuck off, and what did she mean they were arguing over some buried treasure? What fucking treasure? There were so many things that needed to be answered.

Junie went on to explain how she and Wild Bill were madly in love, and how their story ended the day he went to prison.

"But what about when he got out? Did he know? Who all knew?"

Denise turned her back because she knew her face would tell it all. She went into the bathroom acting like she had to pee, when in actuality, she just knew Lexxy wasn't taking this well, and she didn't want to be a part of the problem.

"Everyone just found out, baby. The day you came to the hospital."

Lexxy looked into Cocaine's eyes, and he nodded his head. It was true, all of it.

"When Wild Bill got out, Dutch and I were already together, married, and happy. I couldn't go back to him at that point, and beyond that, Dutch would've killed one of us if not both had he known the truth back then. It just made more sense to keep it a secret."

Lexxy couldn't believe what she was hearing. Denise, from the bathroom, heard everything that was going on and flushed the toilet. She hoped all of Lexxy's questions were done, because now she just wanted to comfort her friend. Denise came out of the bathroom and dried her hands on the paper towels outside of the door, then she walked up to Lexxy and put her arms around her.

"And now? Do you still love him, or was it all just a ploy for money, Mom?"

Junie couldn't believe what her daughter was saying. Everything she'd ever done was for her and Wild Bill. She played nice with Dutch so that Wild Bill could have what he wanted, a way to take care of her, and she stayed with him to keep all of them safe.

"Lexxy, one day, when you have your own children, or someone that you love more than the air you breathe, perhaps it'll be Cocaine, you'll realize that there is nothing, and I do mean NOTHING, that you won't do to see that person be happy and make their dreams come true. I was doing that for Wild Bill. I won't apologize for what I did because I can promise you, you were conceived out of love, but I will apologize for not telling you sooner. I'm sorry, sweetheart, I was just trying to protect you and Bill. I love you both so very much."

Junie had nothing else to say, she didn't know what else to say anyway. She'd finally spoken her truth, and whether or not Lexxy accepted that was up to her. She hoped one day she would forgive her, and she hoped this didn't ruin their relationship completely because she wanted to always be a part of her daughter's life, but she knew this day would come where she would have to pay for her own sins, and judgement day was here.

Junie couldn't stand seeing the look of distraught that covered Lexxy's face, so she turned her back to leave the room. The pressure and tension around them felt like it was coming down in a million different directions.

Before Junie could completely exit the room, Lexxy called out to her. "Mommy?"

Quickly, Junie spun around and looked back at her daughter whose face was covered in tears.

"Yes, baby?"

"I'm pissed, pissed beyond fucking belief, but I'll get over it, and this too shall pass. I can't even begin to imagine what it's like to sacrifice love for safety, so I'm sorry, Mama. I'm sorry, but you should've told me, and I'm going to need time to get over this, to let it go, ok?"

Junie couldn't believe how mature and wise her daughter was. All she could do was smile, and she left the room.

Denise was just glad that her shit didn't spill from her own mouth. She knew eventually she'd have to tell her the truth, but she wasn't as strong as Junie was. Sure, she and Denise were close, but they weren't directly related, and she could cut Denise off if she wanted to, not like her mother, who no matter what, would be her mother for the rest of her life, so she kept that detail to herself and continued comforting her friend, as she had always done.

The tears in the room were forming and falling from everyone's eyes, and Junie couldn't take it. As she sat outside of Lexxy's door, Junie tried reaching out to Dutch one more time. He was being childish now, and this was getting ridiculous. Did she understand the severity of the situation? Of course, but they were all adults, at least she thought they were, and there was no time for all of that to be taking place.

Regardless of the mistake she'd made by keeping a secret this long, he did in fact raise Lexxy, so why wasn't he there with her? Surely, there wasn't enough hurt in the world to keep him away from his little girl, biological or not. Blood don't make you family; it makes you related. It's when we start thinking about shit too much that we take logic too seriously and throw our feelings out of the window, and that's exactly what Dutch was doing.

When he got home, he went back outside, only to find the golden bricks and Trisha were gone. She'd gotten away with how he made his fortune, and now, there would be pay back for stealing from him. As much as he wished he could focus on Lexxy right now, he couldn't. He was so angry at Junie for the lie she told, and mad at Wild Bill for plotting on him, he didn't know who he could trust; and usually, Junie and Wild Bill were the main people he usually trusted, but this, this was terrible.

Dutch walked through the house, looking around the walls, the coffee tables, the kitchen, and all he saw were photos of Lexxy. She was his little girl, but was she?

Everything he felt for her was going out of the window because of the way he was raised. Blood is everything; that's what he was taught. You treat your blood better than you treat others because others didn't come from you, they are not you. That was a philosophy Dutch had always lived by, it was also why he never let Wild Bill make as much money as he could've been making because he wasn't family, not in the blood relation sense anyway.

The calls Junie kept putting into him every few minutes were starting to drive him crazy. He had nothing to say to her, at least nothing that she would want to hear. Everything he had in his mind was evil. He wasn't thinking about anything with a redeeming spirit nor did he have any kind words for her. All of his thoughts were of blood and death, and basic darkness.

When he got his hands on Wild Bill, and he would, when he did, it was simple—he was going to kill him. He couldn't believe Junie was able to keep a secret like this from him, even more so, she kept two secrets. She neglected to tell him that she and Wild Bill were even an item, and she definitely didn't tell him about Wild Bill being the father, so Junie was doing more than Dutch could handle.

Did he want to be at the hospital? More than anything, but he couldn't stomach being around Junie or looking Lexxy in the eye. What would he say to her now that he found out the truth, that he wasn't her father? What would he say to somehow make this ok? He wasn't a wizard; he couldn't snap his fingers and everything go back to how they were before. Even with Wild Bill giving up his kidney, Dutch still wanted him dead. He didn't find him worthy enough to be Lexxy's father, no one was except him, but he was finding it hard for him to be a father or anything at the moment.

If Junie hadn't have kneed him at the hospital, they'd probably still be fighting right now. He wanted to kick her ass all over Nashville for what she'd done. He no longer saw her as his wife, his loving, amazing wife and mother to his child. He saw her as a potential threat and even wondered if she had anything to do with what happened in the backyard. Again, he didn't feel like he could trust anyone, but the incessant noise of his phone ringing was literally driving him up the wall, and he had to either respond or cut the muthafucka off, and cutting it off would be too dangerous, so he went ahead and spoke his peace. He carefully crafted the perfect message to send to Junie, and when he was satisfied, he hit send, and went on about his day. A drug lord never truly gets to sleep, especially when you have people after you. There was a reason Wild Bill, Trisha, and Cocaine were in the back yard—the golden bricks of course, but how did they find them back there? That was the question. It seemed as if Dutch's tight ship he thought he ran, he had been out of touch with for too long. It was time to hit the streets, find Trisha, and of course, get the payback he was now oh so thirsty for.

Junie looked at her phone as the vibration from it nearly made her jump out of her skin. She'd been so busy texting Dutch and calling him, and he wasn't calling her back, but the feeling from the phone scared her half to death because she wasn't expecting it. She knew Dutch could be a brat, but this was going too far. He was going overboard, and Junie just hoped he'd come to his senses soon enough. She hoped that's what this message was about, wanting to be ok with it, or ok at least. She didn't know what the message was going to say. All Junie could do was open it and read it and hope for the best of course.

"Here's the thing, you keep blowin' me up like I'm the one who did something wrong when it was yo' skank ass, so stop calling me. I know what the fuck is going on up there, and just like you, I can call and find out the information I need to know. I'll call Lexxy later myself if I get around to it. She ain't my responsibility no more. That's all you and Bill. You got it."

When Junie first got involved with Dutch, there were many people who told her she shouldn't be involved with him. She was warned that he was a monster, a terrible person, wasn't worth anything but money, but she saw something different inside of him, something that other people clearly didn't see. She hurt on the inside because this Dutch wasn't the Dutch she thought she'd married. She knew he was petty, crazy, childish, but this shit here, this shit had her mind blown.

As Junie was closing out the message, Doctor Graham was coming up beside her.

"Hello, Junie. We've come to get our girl for surgery."

Junie's face instantly lit up. She was so happy to hear this news. She didn't think she'd be feeling as happy as she did in this moment since everything with Dutch that was going on, but she was starting to feel a little better. It was as if she'd taken an emotional Tylenol and it worked right away.

"Wonderful, and how long will this take? How's Bill? He came out alright?"

She didn't really know how to feel. On one hand, of course she was worried about Bill. She always worried about him, but on the other hand, she knew him well enough to know that it would take more than a kidney to get him out of the way. Now that he knew the truth about Lexxy, Junie also knew he'd fight tooth and nail, Heaven and Hell, to make sure he returned to her.

"Bill is doing just fine. He is really a trooper. He woke up almost immediately after we took out the kidney. It scared me a bit--I've never seen anything like it."

Junie knew exactly what Doctor Graham meant. Wild Bill had always been very strong, and sometimes, it even surprised her. When she and Wild Bill were together when they were younger, she remembered him suffering a fatal gunshot wound. While they were operating on him, he wouldn't stay asleep. He was awake for every moment of it. That was another sign letting Junie know just how strong he was. Wild Bill was headstrong, and he had a nice, no, scratch that, amazing body. He was in pretty good health despite all he'd been through in his life. He had a god head on his shoulders but shit usually didn't work out for him. However, Lexxy was his greatest accomplishment, whether he knew it or not. But, as most fathers do, whether they are aware or not, they pine over and even love their daughters more than anyone in the world. More than their wives, their mothers, and even more than their sons.

"Lexxy's surgery could take anywhere from two to four hours just depending, and her recovery time is up to her afterwards. As long as we don't have any complications during the surgery, I'm confident that everything will be just fine, excuse me."

Doctor Graham shook Junie's hand, and he went inside the room with his trusted staff of nurses, including Jo Anne, and they took Lexxy off to hopefully be repaired and restored

An hour or so into the surgery, Denise remembered something she had to do. She promised Lucky she would keep him updated on how she was doing from time to time. Yes, Lucky was not a good boyfriend, but he had been a good friend to Lexxy before they dated, and the fact of the matter was, he still cared about her. He cared deeply for her and wanted to see her be happy and live out her dreams.

Denise stepped away from Cocaine and Junie and called Lucky to let him know where they were. She knew that it would probably cause a problem with Cocaine, but she figured Lexxy wouldn't have a problem with it. She didn't seem too bothered by it the time before, and a promise was a promise.

Lucky had his downfalls, but he wanted to be there for Lexxy if he could be. He wasn't all the way garbage; he just couldn't commit, at least not to Lexxy, not then anyway, but there wasn't a day that went by that he didn't wish he would've done things differently. He wished he would've told Lexxy the truth about Carley and his son. The sad part about it was he didn't cheat on her. There was no infidelity. His son had been conceived before he and Lexxy started dating, but it was Carly's fault for keeping him from his son.

Then, when Carly came into the picture, all Lucky thought about was telling Lexxy, how he should tell Lexxy, and if he should believe the word of a woman he hadn't seen or spoken to in years. His initial reaction was to go and see her just to see how valid this child was. In his mind, the child might not have even really been real. She could've just been lying to get him back. That wouldn't have been unheard of.

He wished he could rewind time and give Lexxy what she wanted to make her happy, but that just wasn't possible. He'd done the worst thing imaginable on accident—kept a secret from her, but he of course wasn't the first person to do so.

Lexxy had so many secrets that she was finding out, and there would only be more to follow.

It didn't take long for Lucky to get to the hospital once Denise made the call. He showed up with a smile on his face and high hopes that the transplant would take. If Lucky could have, he would've given her his kidney plus more. He would've done anything for Lexxy, but when it counted the most to her, he didn't, which ultimately led her to moving on to bigger and better things like Cocaine.

Denise met Lucky at the door, giving him a tight hug. Over the course of a year, a man she couldn't stand had become a close friend, more like a brother really, and she appreciated him being there for her when she felt like she was going to crack. She couldn't talk to her best friend about herself, especially not about her being sick, so Lucky was a good alternative. She didn't want to talk to Cocaine about it because he was so close to the situation, and she didn't want to hurt him. It was just easier for her to talk to Lucky, and he'd been a good listener.

Lucky truly didn't have any ulterior motives. He knew he would never get Lexxy back. No matter what, that wasn't going to happen, so the best and only thing he could do was at least be there. He could show up, and that's all he was trying to do. When Cocaine saw him, his temper flared up faster than it takes a cigarette to light.

"Oh nah, nigga. You gotta get out of here, now!"

"Look, you need to chill, for real. I just came up here to check on her, that's all. I just want to make sure she's ok."

Cocaine couldn't believe the balls on this dude. Why wouldn't he just die? This nigga was like a cockroach, he could survive a nuclear war.

"You wasn't checkin' on her when you was sneakin' around with a woman and a kid, you wasn't checkin' on her when she expected you to man up and give her a ring instead of a key. The fuck you think she need you for when she got me?"

Cocaine jumped up from his seat, heading in Lucky's direction. Denise saw what was about to happen before it even did. She got in the middle to try and diffuse the situation, but Cocaine's fist was already raised, and when he swung, he hit Denise right in the jaw, making blood fly directly from her mouth.

"Damn it, Denise! My bad," Cocaine said as he got to his knees, trying to check on Denise. She hit the floor as soon as Cocaine's fist connected with her cheek. That shit was a straight knock out.

"You shouldn't have been taking up for this nigga. Wait, y'all ain't datin', are you?"

Cocaine wondered, Lucky had been up at the hospital every time something happened with Lexxy, and he knew it was Denise's doing, but was this nigga there because he and Denise were together? That would really fuck Lexxy up, but Cocaine didn't want to accuse her of something, he wanted to know.

Denise massaged her jaw muscle and stared up into Cocaine's eyes.

"No! I would never do that to Lexxy. She's my best friend, my sister, so hell no, I wouldn't do that to her. Why would you think I would?"

"Shit, y'all close and shit. You protectin' this nigga, what else am I supposed to think?"

"I wasn't protectin' him! I was tryin' to dead the situation before something like this happened. Granted, I didn't think it would be me to get hit."

Cocaine was always accidentally doing some shit. He always thought with his heart and not his head, which made him do some stupid shit, ninety-nine percent of the time.

"I'm so, so sorry, but that nigga needs to go!" Cocaine roared.

Denise turned around and stood in front of Lucky. "To avoid this situation from getting any worse, maybe we need to all just cool it. Cocaine, let him stay until he can see Lexxy for himself. I know you don't want to say it's cool, but is it really worth it to stir up trouble and upset anyone else? Seems like it's already pretty tense in here."

Cocaine had to admit, Denise was making sense, he just hated that they were in a hospital because if they weren't, he would've flipped the fuck out on this nigga just like he had accidentally done on Denise.

"Fine, but after that, that nigga gotta go."

Lucky smiled, he hadn't been defeated. Though he didn't come to cause trouble, he loved knowing that he made Cocaine uncomfortable, like his position was threatened, even though deep down, he knew Lexxy didn't want to be with him, and they would never reconcile in a romantic way.

Lexxy was wheeled into her room in a bed, and her eyes were open. She'd been awake for some time now but said she didn't want to see anyone. She needed a moment to finish processing everything that had happened in just one day. Somehow, some way, the cords in her room had been unplugged, Wild Bill was her father, and Dutch had disappeared before she even had a chance to talk to him. She could understand him being mad at Junie but not made enough to stay away from seeing her when she was going through something herself, but then she felt selfish for even having that thought.

She was so thankful that someone from above was looking out for her. The doctor said the transplant was a success so far, but they needed to keep her for a little while to monitor the kidney's behavior and make sure her body could take it.

After a six hour operation, with recovery time included, all Lexxy wanted to do was sleep, but she knew after making her family wait for so long to see her, they'd want to know how she was doing, so she was ready to get it over with, but it was strange, the main people she needed to see, she couldn't. She wanted to see Wild Bill so she could thank him, and of course, so she could chew his ass out for not telling her about having been with her mother, she wanted to see Dutch to apologize because she didn't know, but she still felt bad. She felt like it was her job to fix this whole situation; she just didn't know how. Lexxy was a problem solver by nature, so the simple fact that she had no solution to any of this ate her alive.

Junie, Cocaine, Denise, and surprisingly enough for Lexxy, Lucky walked in the room. When she saw him, a loud sigh left her mouth. She knew he shouldn't be here, and now, after all this time, she realized why it was inappropriate, and how it probably made Cocaine feel uncomfortable, even though he would never actually use the word "uncomfortable," because in all honesty, she felt the same exact way.

She'd mourned their relationship, she cried many, many nights, and she was finally over it. There was nothing holding her back from being happy with Cocaine, and she needed Lucky to stop popping up in her presence. She appreciated his concern, but she didn't know why Denise did this a second time.

"Uhm…Lucky, what are you doing here?" were the first words she spoke, even before speaking to Cocaine, though she of course noticed him, and it was hard to miss the look of sheer anger that was flatly painted on his face.

"I wanted to come check on you. Denise told me what happened. I asked her to keep me updated, and here I am. If I could've given you my kidney, I would have."

"Pshhhh." Cocaine couldn't believe this dude. He was coming on way too strong, but really, he was just being too damn corny for Cocaine's liking.

Lucky looked up at Cocaine, who he felt was acting like a child, but he imagined he'd feel the same way if the roles were reversed.

"Well, that's cool and all, Lucky, but I wouldn't have taken it because I would feel like I always owed you something, and I don't want to feel indebted to anyone. For real, for real, you shouldn't even be here. Denise, I understand, you were trying to be nice, and even be friendly, but I don't even want him here. Lucky, this is so inappropriate."

Denise thought she was doing what Lexxy would want her to do, but then she realized maybe it was just what she wanted. She was being selfish and not thinking of what Lexxy might have wanted, instead, she was thinking of herself.

"I'm sorry, Lex. I really am. This has been really hard on me, and Lucky has been there for me through all of this. I really am sorry."

"I bet you are, and I mean that with no shade attached to it. It's fine. Just go, Lucky, thank you for checking on me."

Lucky didn't know what to say, but he knew he needed to get to steppin' before Cocaine said anything or did something worse than anything he could've possibly said. Everything was happening so fast, but it also seemed to be moving in slow motion. Hearing those words from Lexxy's mouth literally echoed in his mind, slowly, and over, and over again.

Even after he left, he kept hearing them in his mind. He basically felt like she never wanted to see him again, but he didn't know how he was going to do that. How was he supposed to just completely walk away from the love of his life? He didn't know, but he had no choice. These were the cards that had finally been dealt out to him, and he would just have to take it and let it go. He loved Lexxy and would give her anything, even if that meant never seeing her again.

Cocaine was happy that Lexxy finally was taking their relationship more seriously and that she handled him so he didn't have to, especially since he'd failed miserably so far.

Cocaine didn't want to talk; there was nothing else to say. His baby was out of surgery, doing well, and everything else could wait. Her health and life were the most important things for now, and they would definitely get to have the wedding Cocaine dreamed of having with his beautiful bride.

CHAPTER 7

Lucky trudged home in defeat. The brief moment he was with Lexxy was like having heaven snatched away from you once you're about to finally start enjoying it. He hated Cocaine, and the fact that he was in Lexxy's life meant that there was no way Lucky could ever get back to her. From what Denise had told him, they were engaged, soon to be married, and Lucky couldn't help but think that that could have been him.

Though he was happy with his new girlfriend, Carley, and their son, he never felt as comfortable with her as he did with Lexxy. This whole dynamic was still new to him. He loved being around his son, and he enjoyed spending time with him, and he even had grown to care for Carley.

When Lucky first came into the picture, he said he wasn't ready for a relationship and that he wanted to take it as slow as possible, but being a father took precedence, and the more time he spent driving back and forth between his house and Carley's, it just took too much time, and then he could only stay for a night or two, and he'd have to be back at home for work. Though Carley didn't ask this of Lucky, he still had them move into his house, so that he could build a bond between his son and himself, and of course, get to know the adult Carley much better.

His son was becoming a young man, and he wanted to rear and instruct him in the proper way. He loved his own father, but after his break up with Lexxy, he realized his teachings about women wasn't right and that he allowed his father to subconsciously ruin and sabotage his relationship with Lexxy. He wouldn't do that again, not with the mother of his child.

If there was anyone he wanted it to work with more than with Lexxy, it was with Carley. He couldn't say he loved her yet, but he definitely had feelings for her, and he would be devastated if she left him, especially since recently, their relationship had been rocky. She was always getting jealous or feeling insecure of everything he did and everyone he was around, which was why he didn't tell her where he was going before he left the house, but he was returning somewhat late, later than he normally would, and he'd either have to make up a lie as to why he was out that long, or he could tell her the truth and face her wrath.

He thought about how he lied to Lexxy about going out of town when he was going to see his son, and he vowed he would never lie again, at least not unless it was during a dire situation.

As he pulled up to his house, he could hear Carley in his mind bitching at him before he even got to the door because he knew how she could be. She didn't play games with him.

Carley was sweet and beautiful, but sweet and beautiful often translated to crazy, and though he had never seen her get too crazy, he had often seen the look in her eye that said there was something behind them that could come out and fuck him up.

Lucky cut off his car and made his way into the house. As soon as he closed the door, he saw his son sliding across the floor, running to jump on him.

"Dad! Dad! I gotta tell you something!"

Lucky reached down to allow his son to jump into his arms. Though he wasn't a little baby, Lucky had missed those days of him being a baby, so it was always like he was working backwards. He was always trying to relive the old days when he wasn't around, so he often still cradled his son, let him sit in his lap, and he even still kissed him like he was a baby.

"Oh, yeah? What's that?" Lucky asked, just as excited as Zeke had initially said it.

"I passed my Math quiz. Remember, the one you helped me study for?"

Lucky was so proud of him. He had been helping Zeke with his Math test for the last few weeks. He knew he was nervous about it because he wasn't a good tester, and Math just wasn't his subject.

"What did you get?" Lucky asked with a smile on his face.

"98! I got two points off..." Zeke's voice trailed off, and in Lucky's mind, he didn't give a shit. All he heard was that he passed, and with a ninety-eight at that. He couldn't have been prouder.

"You, my man, just earned yourself some ice cream after dinner."

"Yes!" Zeke jumped up and down and ran into the kitchen.

"Zeke, boy, you better stop running in my house!" Carley yelled from the kitchen. Lucky had text her and told her he'd be home somewhat late, and she didn't play that eating before Lucky came home. She believed in family, and if the entire family wasn't eating, no one was going to eat, unless it was an emergency, or if it was going to be way too late.

Carley came out of the kitchen wearing leggings, a t-shirt, and her favorite apron. She truly loved to cook, and she had different aprons designated for different times and days, and sometimes even different occasions.

"Mmmm....so you finally decided to bring your ass home. Where you been? I know you wasn't at work; I called your job."

Lucky backed up. He was prepared to greet her with a hug and a kiss, but now, he didn't even feel like it. This was the type of shit he was talking about, that insecure shit that he couldn't stand.

"No, I wasn't at work. I never said I was going to be working late, only that I would be home late."

Zeke slid into the chair, and Carley took off her apron and threw it on the table.

"That's why I'm askin' you. Where the fuck you been at?" she asked with her hand on her hip and her head tightly tilted.

Lucky didn't want to lie, but he didn't feel like he owed her an explanation, but to keep the peace, he decided to just go ahead and tell her because she wouldn't let it go otherwise.

"I went to go and see Lexxy. She was finally able to get her kidney, but before that, she had some type of accident, so I wanted to make sure she was ok."

"Why? That ain't your job. She ain't your responsibility anymore. The sooner you realize that, the better. Let me find out you're trying to get back with your ex, I promise you won't see me and Zeke ever again."

In that moment, Lucky didn't give a damn if he ever saw her again. He just wanted to be with his son, but he didn't want to argue with Carley. It was just way too much, and she always had a way of making him feel worse.

"You right, baby. I just wanted to make sure she was straight one last time, and I'm good now. At one point, I had a lot of feelings for her, and I just needed, for my own sanity, to make sure she was cool. Don't be mad at me, baby. I'm sorry."

Lucky approached Carley with his arms open, and he laid a juicy kiss on her lips, hoping that would cool her jets for the evening. When she wrapped her arms around his waist, he knew he got her.

"Good, I'm glad you understand what I was sayin'. If I find out you was around that bitch again though, Lucky, I'ma make you regret it. I promise."

For some reason, Lucky could tell that she really meant that, and he didn't want to play with fire and get burnt. Lucky and Carley sat down with Zeke to eat their meal, and even though Lucky agreed to stay away from her, he had no intentions on really doing so, but he would keep quiet for now and try to keep what he was planning on the downlow. He knew he'd never get Lexxy back, but it didn't hurt to try, right?

The next day, Lexxy woke up feeling stronger than she had in some time. She normally felt weak when she first got up or like she wasn't up for the day, but she woke up with strength and a clear head, something she hadn't felt in a long time.

"Good morning, Sexxy Lexxy. How you feelin', baby?"

She looked over and saw Cocaine who hadn't left her side the entire time.

"I feel great, like I'm ready to get up and start walking."

"Woah, woah, let's not go overboard, let's take it slow. If you want to take a small walk around the room, that's fine, but we not gettin' in the hallway until I know you can handle it."

Lexxy rolled her eyes at how overprotective Cocaine was, but what else could she expect? Cocaine had been by her side this entire time, and she knew he would never leave her. They'd been through so much together, and there would be more to come, but Lexxy knew as long as they were together, none of that mattered. She had finally found the man she was going to spend the rest of her life with. Too bad she wasted so much time on

Lucky's ass. She often wondered if she would have let him go before if God would've blessed her with another man, a better man—Cocaine, but now, that didn't really matter. She was fortunate to have the man she did have, and she would never, ever let him go. As long as he would have her, she would have him, and they would be happy, together.

"Fine, let's do it."

It had been a long time since strength coursed through her veins, and she wanted to feel what that strength was like. She wanted to be normal again, and slowly, but surely, she felt like it was about to start happening. Lexxy pulled the covers off her body and wrapped her hand around the IV machine so she could get her walk on. Cocaine rushed to the other side of the bed and grabbed her arm.

"Here, baby, lean on me."

Lexxy held one of Cocaine's arms and the IV machine and pulled herself out of the bed. She didn't realize how heavy she'd feel, but when her feet touched the ground, they felt like bricks. Though she was feeling good, she felt like her body wouldn't move, at least not one step passed the bed.

"Not as easy as you thought, huh?" Cocaine joked with Lexxy, and for the first time in a while, he saw that same glowing smile he'd fallen in love with. Lately, when she smiled, it seemed forced with sadness behind her eyes, but this, this was who she truly was.

Lexxy began by scooting across the floor, barely picking her feet up. Cocaine figured it would take her time to be able to readjust to having this much weight on her legs, so he was patient and steady with her. He was just happy to be able to hold her in his arms again. All the time she spent in the chair and then again in the hospital bed was somewhat overwhelming, and he missed lying with his Lexxy at night, holding and kissing her, making her feel safe. He could protect her against the world, but he had no control over what her body did, and that drove him insane.

As Cocaine walked Lexxy around the room, a knock broke Lexxy's concentration, almost bringing her to the ground, but Cocaine had her, as he always did.

"Steady, baby. I got you."

He grabbed ahold of her waist and pulled her closer to him so she wouldn't fall.

"Yes, I have a delivery for a Lexxy. Is that you, ma'am?"

Lexxy looked up, feeling confused. Who would be sending her something?

"Yes, that's me. Who is the delivery from?"

"Doesn't say, but there is a card inside. We're not allowed to read them, so here you go."

The man came in with a vase of yellow tulips, Lexxy's favorite, a bag of Goldfish, with a note attached to it. Cocaine walked Lexxy over to her bed and helped her sit down, and he helped the delivery man bring the items inside. Cocaine signed for the delivery, and then the man left.

"Mmm....let me find out you got a secret admirer, baby. He gon' be dead fuckin' with me."

Lexxy knew there was a lot of truth to that. Whoever it was knew her well enough to know that she loved

Goldfish; it was her favorite snack, and instead of roses to get tulips, specifically yellow ones.

Cocaine pulled the note out and began reading over it, and as soon as he was done, he crumpled it up and threw it in the trash can, his fingers almost singing the paper between his fingers.

"Baby, what's wrong?"

"What's wrong is that nigga, Lucky. You know what, I'm 'bout to go handle his bitch ass, 'cuz he don't seem like he like to listen to reason too good."

"Baby, wait," Lexxy said as she rose from the bed and then hit the floor. Cocaine was so mad, he didn't even realize she slapped the floor until he heard her groaning.

"Baby, come on now. You gotta be careful. What you doin'?"

"I'm tryna stop you from acting out. So what he sent a gift? We can throw it in the trash. He already knows this shit ain't cool, so who gives a fuck? You gotta stop gettin' so upset before you bust a blood vessel. You gotta just relax, daddy."

Cocaine's eyebrows went up when Lexxy called him daddy, something she normally only did during sex, but it always turned him on whenever he heard it, and this time was no different. If Lexxy hadn't have been so weak, he would've bent her over right there and punished her pussy. Punished her for not tellin' that nigga to step off before now, and punished her because she needed it.

"I ain't the insecure type, baby, but I am a get it done type of nigga. You want me to keep a level head, text that nigga and let him know what's up. Let him know he can't send you shit, he can't call, he can't text, he can't come near you. None of that. Let him know, lil' baby, or I will."

Lexxy knew he was not joking, and once she was able to get back in the bed and get her phone, which Cocaine retrieved almost immediately for her once she was back comfortable, she sent Lucky a final goodbye, letting him know that this had to stop. Regardless of how he was feeling or how much he wanted to be there, he just couldn't.

Lexxy thought about what she should say, and then she began typing the message out to him.

"Lucky, I don't know how many times I can make it clear. It is inappropriate for us to be in contact in any shape, form, or fashion. It is inappropriate for you to send gifts that I can't and will not accept. It is just inappropriate, everything you do. Please leave me alone completely. This is the last time I'ma tell you."

Lexxy hit the send button, and even though she felt bad for having to say it like that, she had to let it go. Lucky was a part of her past, and she just wanted him to stay there to save his own life. If he was smart, then he would do as she told him to do because Cocaine wasn't playing, and just as soon as Lexxy was better, there would be nothing to hold Cocaine back or stop him from fucking some shit up.

Lucky sat on the couch checking his messages for the morning. He couldn't wait to see the thank you Lexxy would probably send him for remembering the things she liked. Unfortunately, that wasn't the case. When he saw Lexxy's name pop up on his phone, he couldn't have been happier. He thought for sure she was going to at least send him a smiley face or a thank you, some happy shit, but what he read almost brought him to tears. Lexxy was really pushing him away.

He read over the text several times before he closed it. He couldn't believe she was saying this to him, why was she saying this? It was all because of Cocaine. Cocaine had changed Lexxy, somehow manipulated her into believing that she didn't want anything to do with him. How was this possible? Lucky didn't realize he was the problem, that he was imagining and making certain things up. Lucky truly thought, at least a part of him thought, he could win back her love and trust, but that wasn't true. Lexxy was done with his ass, and she wanted him to move on, but there was no one who wanted him to move on more than Carley.

Blind to what was going on around him, Carley was

standing right behind him reading the damn text message that he kept scrolling up and down, up and down. She had been standing behind him a good five minutes, and he would've never even known had she not made her presence obvious.

Carley swung her hand back behind her as high as she could, and she brought the wrath of the gods down on his head.

"WHAP! WHAP! WHAP!"

"Nigga, have you lost your damn mind? See, I knew this shit was gon' happen! I fucking knew it!"

"Ow, Carley, stop, what the fuck is ya' problem?"

"You are! You're my problem. I told you last night, but obviously you wasn't listening. Leave. That Bitch. Alone!"

Carley swung her hand back again and BOOM! Her hand swaddled the side of his face, leaving a red print of her hand on it. Lucky jumped off the couch, running behind it, staring at Carley with his chest poking out, breathing heavily.

"I don't give a fuck about you breathing all hard. I wish you would put ya' hands on me, puta! You know what, I was coming in here to confront yo' ass because I saw the charge on your online statement that you bought a "Get Well" gift, and I knew it wasn't for my ass. You spent one-hundred dollars on that bitch! Hell, I can't even get you to spend that type of money on me at one time. I swear to God, Lucky, you don't have no more chances. This is the end for ya' stupid ass. If you can't get it together, I'ma leave you! I saw the message she sent you. That girl don't want you! She don't want yo' ass, why can't you get that through your fuckin' head? Maybe I need to smack you a few more times."

Carley raised her hand like she was about to hit him again, but this time, he grabbed her by the wrists and pushed her against the dresser that sat in front of the wall.

"Carley, if you ever put yo' hands on me again, I'ma whoop yo' ass like you a nigga on the street. I mean that with everything in my body. I ain't never been disrespected like this!"

"Did I hear you correctly? Did you say disrespect? You couldn't have! You been disrespecting me all this time, and I'm supposed to just go along with it? No! I will fuck you up. Now this my last time warning you. Next time, it's not gon' play out this way, now let me go."

Carley broke free of Lucky's grip, and as she walked away, she wondered why she even put up with his shit. Carley was beautiful. She had long, wavy hair. Big, full lips that were pink and supple. Her body was on full attack, C-cup breasts, a small but juicy booty, and the bitch even had abs, not to mention she had some good head. Lucky was tripping and going to miss out on this amazing woman. She was crazy and insecure, but she had a reason to be. She felt the way she felt for a reason. She wasn't making this shit up, and she knew she wasn't, but Lucky had her fucked up if he didn't think she wouldn't leave him.

The sad thing was, they hardly even had sex anymore, another thing that attributed to Carley's insecurities. She wondered what was holding him back because they used to hump like crazy—protected and unprotected, but out of the blue, it just stopped. She didn't want to believe it was because he was still pressed about Lexxy, but now, her suspicions were confirmed, and if Lucky was smart, which he wasn't, but if he was, he would've continued having sex with her to keep her cool, but that wasn't about to happen tonight.

Lucky wasn't a killer, but he was so close to ending Carley's life for putting her hands on him repeatedly. This wasn't the first time something like this had happened. Carley was always throwing blows around the house, and sometimes, even in public. Lucky usually let her slide, but he was tired of her shit.

Thankfully, Zeke was still in the bed. He hated fighting in front of his son because he didn't want Zeke to think that that was how you loved your woman. He was taught a different way, but he knew what his father did was wrong, and he wanted the best life for his son, but Carley made it damn hard for him not to flip the fuck out on her.

If he couldn't have Lexxy back, he would stay with Carley, but he still had one major trick up his sleeve that he hadn't pulled yet. He heard Carley, but Carley didn't understand; he loved Lexxy, and she was at one point his world. He didn't see himself loving Carley the way he loved Lexxy, and she just needed to accept that. She was trying to force her feelings on him, and this was the type of shit that made him run away, but he was done running from Lexxy. He wanted to run towards Lexxy and into her arms. He wanted them to get back together, get married, have children, and just be happy together. It had been too long since he'd been with his baby, but he was about to make a comeback, no matter who didn't like it.

THREE WEEKS LATER...

"Hallelujah! Get me the fuck up out of here!" Lexxy yelled as she ran into Cocaine's arms. She had completely gotten the feeling back in her legs, and they no longer felt like bricks. If anything, she felt lighter than she ever had, and this time, she was walking out of the hospital, no matter what the doctors or the nurses had to say. She wasn't going to be stuck in that wheelchair or stuck in any chair, ever again.

"Let's go, lil' baby."

Cocaine reached for Lexxy's hand, and he walked her out the front door to the car. They were finally about to be able to get their lives started, and it was crazy. No matter what had been thrown at them, they stayed together and were happy, something most couples didn't know how to do. Under pressure, they stood together, and this was the kind of relationship Lexxy always wanted.

She needed Cocaine more than he even knew, and she was really about to need him because she was about to ask him to do something he definitely wasn't going to want to do.

Once Cocaine closed the door to the car after Lexxy got in, he jogged to the other side, closed the door, cranked the car up, and got some music going.

"I'm walkin' on sunshine, wow! I'm walkin' on sunshine, and don't it feel good!"

Lexxy's head bobbed along with the music as her favorite song played through the radio, but her excitement dwindled quickly once she realized they were headed to their home, when they needed to be going to Dutch's house, but she'd forgotten to mention it.

"Wait, baby, I wanna go see my dad, Dutch, whatever. He's still like my dad too. I need to go see him."

Cocaine hit the brakes so fast. He couldn't believe what he was hearing. He thought it was great that Dutch had finally disappeared from their lives, but now that Lexxy was mentioning it, he didn't want to be upset, but he couldn't help it. Any day now, he'd be retrieving the golden bricks from Trisha, and he and Lexxy were finally about to get rid of this dude. Why did she want to see him?

"Coco, cut the dramatics, slamming on the brakes like you done lost your mind. Listen to me, I know how you feel about him and how he feels about you, but this shit has gotten way out of control. With everything that's been happening recently, if we've learned anything, it's gotta be that tomorrow isn't promised, and I don't want him to leave up out of this world thinking I don't care about him. I already told Mom we were coming over, so turn the car around, and let's go."

Cocaine couldn't argue with that, but like a small

child, he wanted to throw a fit, to tell her he wasn't going to take her, but he knew he couldn't do that. He couldn't just have a fit in the car or at all; he was a grown man, and grown men didn't act the way that he was feeling. Plus, he would do anything for Lexxy, and if she wanted to go see Dutch, he would take her to do so, he just wasn't going to go in. He already knew how that was going to end, and he was tired of fighting. He was tired of seeking revenge when it kept turning up empty.

Cocaine took the long drive up the driveway, and what seemed like thirty minutes later, he was able to get through the gate of course with the help of Lexxy and park in front of the house.

"If you're not out in thirty minutes, I'm coming to get you, baby. I'm not tryna be out here all day. I wanna get you home and do some nasty shit."

Lexxy giggled and agreed. She felt the same way. She wanted to do the same thing to him. She couldn't wait to feel her man's dick in her mouth and all over her body. She even wanted to rub it on her face.

As Lexxy walked up to the door of the house she grew up in, she heard yelling before she could even open the door.

"You a hoe, and your ways is hoe-ish. If you wanna be with that nigga, go ahead, get the fuck out of here. I'm sure he's at home waiting for you to suck his dick like you used to!" Dutch yelled from the top of the stairs.

Lexxy walked in the house and saw her mother downstairs and Dutch upstairs, and they were engaged in a huge fight.

"A hoe? I don't know why you keep saying that. I

didn't cheat on you, I didn't betray you, if anything, I've always been on your side. If I wanted, I could've gone back to Wild Bill when he got out of prison, but I didn't. I remained your wife, kept your secrets, loved you, and even put up with your shit!"

"Shit, I already told you, you can go. You ain't gotta be here. Matter of fact, you can go, now!"

Dutch went into the master bedroom, and when he returned, he had Junie's expensive clothes, shoes, her jewelry, everything she owned, and he started throwing it over the bannister.

"Mom, what the hell is going on in here?"

Junie shifted her weight and turned around to see her daughter. She didn't want her to see this or even know about it. If she and Dutch were going to split up, she would've pretended to be happy, she would've pretended that everything was ok, but not now. Dutch had become too disrespectful and was clearly losing his mind.

"Your father—"

"I ain't ya' daddy, but I know you already know that."

"Woah, don't take a shot at me. I haven't done anything to you!"

Lexxy's face now held a scowl on it. She couldn't believe the things that were coming out of his mouth. In all the years she'd been alive, she never heard him speak to her mother this way, and he definitely never spoke to her that way. She understood that he was hurt; hell, she was too, but this was out of control.

"Here! You can take it all with you wherever you're going. I guess you had ya' daughter come and pick you up because you know yo' ass can't stay here!"

"No, she was on her way to come and see you, to speak with you. If I would've known you were going to start cutting up today, I would've told her to stay where she was or to go home with Cocaine!"

"Oh, yeah. Go home with Cocaine. Go home with your traitorous ass boyfriend, and you can go home to your man. I'm done with your ass. If I gotta have you escorted off the premises, I swear I will."

"I dare you to try!"

"'Mom, don't push it. Why don't we just get your stuff and go home? This is too much for one day."

"Home? This is my home!"

Lexxy tried to grab her mother, but she stepped away before she could even get close enough.

"Daddy, Daddy! Stop trippin'. You can't do this to Mom!"

"Your hoe ass mama did this to herself."

Every few minutes that passed by, more items were thrown downstairs, but Junie didn't even care. If this was truly the end of her marriage, she didn't want to take anything that reminded her of the past. She didn't want anything from this fucked up relationship. She knew the end of her marriage was coming, but she didn't think it would end like this, or at least she hoped for as much.

She hated this was happening in front of Lexxy; once again, her world was being turned upside down, but damn, this was more than it simply being turned upside down, this was about to be a new life.

Lexxy had never seen Dutch act this way, and she could literally feel the hurt in his words, and she saw it in his face. He was crying. His words were broken by the sniffling of tears and the eruption of saliva in his throat, and there was no way Lexxy was going to let her mother go and stay in the guest house or in some hotel.

"Mama, come on. You can come home with me and Cocaine. Don't worry about anything."

"I'm not worried. I'm upset by how this turned out. I'm sorry about this. I'm sorry how all of this turned out."

"Don't worry about that right now, Mama. I don't give a damn. I don't like how he's talking to your or treating you. No matter what you did, you don't deserve to be thrown out like some outcast. Let's leave here with some dignity. Fuck these clothes—that's all they are anyway. Let's just leave."

Thank God Junie had her own money. She wouldn't have to rely on the money from her husband, even though she had plenty of it. She was smart enough to save for just in case something happened. A little of her money and a little of his went a long way. Junie didn't want to impose on her daughter, but where else was she going to go? She wouldn't dare go and stay with Wild Bill, even though that option was available to her, and she knew it, but she really didn't want to stay with her daughter. She was just getting her life back, and she didn't want to disturb it anymore than it already had been.

"Come on, Mama. Let's go!"

Lexxy grabbed Junie's arm, Junie grabbed her purse, and she walked out of them with nothing but the clothes on her back, her money, and the wedding ring her husband gave her over twenty years ago. She'd always valued it and appreciated it, and she always would, whether she was Dutch's woman or not.

When Lexxy and Junie got outside to the car, Cocaine didn't understand what was going on. He assumed Lexxy was coming over for a visit, but he didn't think they'd be taking any ridealongs.

"Hey, Mama, how's everything?"

Cocaine fixed the mirror to look at Junie, and she looked like she was in distress. Like she was almost sick.

"Cocaine, just drive and take us home. Mama's gon' stay with us for a little while." Lexxy plopped herself back in her seat and propped her feet up on the dashboard.

"No, no, I just need some time to cool down, I'll be out of your hair by tonight."

"Damn it, Mama, if you don't put that pride away, you betta! You're staying with us, and that's that."

"Well, do you need some clothes—"

"Cocaine, just drive!" Lexxy yelled. She was furious, and she was starting to see that monster that she'd been hearing so much about inside of Dutch. This shit was beyond out of control, but Lexxy was going to be there for her mother. Regardless of her mistake, she would never leave her stranded and lonely the way Dutch was doing. She wasn't going to disown her. She was going to continue loving her, and hopefully, one day, things would be ok. She needed them to get better sooner rather than later because she would eventually be getting married, and she wanted Dutch to be there. Biological father or not, he was still her dad, and it was time for him to start acting like it again.

"Ow...that hurts, Dutch. Stop, Dutch! You're hurting me!"

"Ok, ok, I hear you. I'm almost done."

Dutch was thrusting inside of Trisha, loving on her like he'd been doing for the last year or so. Dutch was always rough with her, way too rough, and she couldn't handle his girth along with how hard he liked to go, but she loved him, so she let him fuck her however he wanted until it became unbearable.

Trisha had fallen in love with him when she first got put down in the gorilla gang, but he paid her no attention, so like any other woman would, she started making her presence known by being in the same places he was, showing off her body, trying to turn him on, and one day, it worked! He actually fell for what she was kickin' to him, and since then, she'd been hooked on him. Hooked on his love, how kind he could be, how crazy he could be, all types of shit, but all of that came to an end the day Junie said she was going to stop traveling so much for work.

"Uhn! Damn, every time I fuck you, it gets better and better."

Dutch climbed off of Trisha and went into the bathroom to start the shower. He had to get home before Junie came back into town, and her flight was scheduled to land in an hour, but he couldn't stand not having a piece of his Trisha. He knew she wasn't fucking anybody else, which made her his, but tonight, he had to break if off with her, and it wasn't going to be pretty. He was prepared for it to be some bullshit, but he hoped it wouldn't come back to bite him in the ass.

While Dutch was in the bathroom taking off his clothes, he stepped into the shower and started lathering his body with soap. Trisha, no matter how much pain she was in, could never get enough of him, so she climbed into the shower with him and grinded her soft body against his. Dutch began kissing on her neck and he placed his hands on her breasts, yanking on her nipples, but she loved it. He bent her over, and she thought he was going to slide into her pussy and beat it up again, instead, he did the thing she loved most, slowly slid into her ass. This always made her cum instantly.

This was the first time he'd ever been somewhat gentle with her, and she noticed that he wasn't killing her ass like he normally did, so she knew something was wrong.

"Dutch, what's going on?"

"Shh…don't say nothin'," he whispered from behind her. He didn't want to hear her say one word. He knew this would be the last time he ever got to tap that ass again, and he wanted it to be the best he could have, and her talking would only ruin his train of thought.

Trisha had one arm up on the shower wall and one leg up on the side of the tub, taking it in her ass like a pro, but she was getting it on both ends. Dutch's hand had migrated down to the front of her pussy and started rubbing her swollen, wet clit.

"Mmm…damn, baby. I love you, Dutch."

Sadly, he loved Trisha too, but he would never tell her that. He admired the way she fought in the streets but was the perfect slut for him, and she did everything he told her to. She was the perfect side piece, and she knew how to keep quiet, but it would only be a matter of time before somebody got to talking too much and told their business, so he had to end it that night.

Together, they came, exploding with one another, something they'd never done at the same time.

"Wooh, shit, girl you be wearin' me out."

Dutch loved fucking her, but this shit was gon' ruin his life.

After they fucked for the last time, he went back to washing himself, and Trisha grabbed a wash cloth and began doing the same.

While she was washing her body, she admired Dutch and how handsome he was. She loved every inch of his body, and she was ready for round three, but as soon as she began lifting her leg to show her perfectly shaved pussy, Dutch pushed it down, and he knew it was time for him to be honest.

"Trisha, I need to tell you something…"

"Ok," she said as she began backing up. She could tell by the tone in his voice something wasn't quite right.

"Listen, Junie will be coming home soon, so I need you to hear what I'm about to say, and I need you to understand. You know how I feel about you, and we've had a lot of fun, but—"

"Say less. I already know what you about to say. I understand. I know this was all supposed to just be fun. It's cool. No worries. As a matter of fact, I'm about to go ahead and get up out of here… you cool with checkin' out?"

Dutch couldn't believe how cool Trisha was being, and he thought it was a trick, but he thought more of Trisha. She wasn't the type to get her panties in a bunch and complain. She usually kept it cool and kept it moving, so he would do the same. This was their usual hotel room, so it was no biggie; when they were ready to leave, they could go.

"Yeah, I got it."

"Cool, stay up!"

Trisha grabbed her clothes and slid them on as quickly as she possibly could. Though in front of Dutch she seemed to have it all together, she was really falling apart inside. Her heart was broken. She knew Dutch would never leave Junie for her. He'd never promised her anything of the sort, but she also never thought he'd cut her off either. They had something special, something worth having, at least she thought they did. She didn't think she was just a booty call, and in all honesty, she wasn't. Dutch really did have feelings for her, but he also loved him some Junie, and he would never do anything to upset her.

But that was two years ago, and the main reason why Trisha was willing to help Cocaine when he approached her in the bar that night. She wanted revenge. She wanted him to feel how she felt when he broke it off with her because she was broken, left damaged and hurt.

But several weeks had gone by since she'd been shot, and no one was looking for her, which was strange, or if they were looking for her, they were doing a horrible job of trying to find her because she wasn't really hiding out that much. She went to one of the guys in the gang who handled gunshot wounds in the field; she wasn't going to the hospital, that would've left her entirely too exposed, but she trusted her gang members, and even though she was on some foul shit, a lot of them still hoped that one day, the gorilla gang would be restored back to its former power and glory with the Blackwood family, so when they found out Trisha tried to steal from Dutch and was actually successful, they stood by her, but now, the silence was deafening, and she needed to know what was on Dutch's mind. She wondered if he wanted to kill her as bad as she wanted to hurt him because if so, she figured she'd be found by now, and she knew how he was. The best thing she could do for herself was try to find out.

But the streets were talking, and they were saying that he and Junie had split, which was exactly what Trisha wanted to hear. She'd been waiting for Junie to either die or leave his ass for a long time so she could have her man back. Cocaine was the closest thing she'd ever had to some good dick after Dutch, but even then, she couldn't compare it to him, and she missed his rough ways, that was the only way she could feel anything was if he was ripping her guts out. For the last two years, she'd felt dead inside, but it was time for her to try and get her man back, but first, she had to take the bricks to Cocaine.

He instructed her to leave them at a location where he would have full surveillance watching to make sure everything was cool before he came to pick them up. After all the hell he raised with Lexxy about Lucky and shit being inappropriate, he realized it was inappropriate for him to be around Trisha now, seeing as how they had fucked, whether they were just working together or not.

Trisha agreed to drop them off, but she said she wasn't going to stay and wait for someone to come and check the bag out. She was ready to go on about her business because she had plans to check up on her man.

After she dropped the gold off, she hopped in her car, and before she could talk herself out of it, she called Dutch. She didn't think he would answer, or if he did, he'd have an attitude, but he didn't. He actually sounded normal.

"Trisha, that you?" Dutch asked as he looked at his phone.

"Yeah, baby, it's me. I'm just....I wanted to call and check on you. I heard about you and Junie."

"Is that what you called for, or did you call to apologize?"

Trisha needed to think quickly. She didn't want to apologize because she didn't really feel bad for what she had done. If anything, she still felt like he deserved it, but she would apologize if that was what he wanted or required to get back in his good graces.

"Is that what you want, daddy? For me to apologize?"

"It would be nice to hear considering you robbed me, little girl."

Whenever Dutch called her little girl, it made her panties wet, something about him being an older man did something to her young pussy, and she loved it.

"I'm sorry, daddy. I am. I was just trying to get your attention. You weren't being bothered with me, and it hurt me. Will you forgive me?"

Dutch laughed. He could use a release, and Trisha was the perfect person to give it to him.

"Of course daddy forgives you. Where are you?"

"I'm out in Cool Springs, on my way home."

"Mmm...go get a hotel, and I'ma meet you there. I got some punishing to do on your ass, and you gon' take it as hard as I give it to you tonight."

"I sure will, daddy, whatever you want."

"Good, text me with the address, and I'll be on the way."

Trisha ended the call with electricity moving all over her body. She couldn't wait to see Dutch and feel him inside of her. She loved him, and she was finally about to get him back. Two years was too long not to be with the person you loved, and now that Junie was out of the picture, there was nothing stopping them from being together.

Dutch came into the hotel room smiling. He truly had missed Trisha, even though he was disappointed in her for what she had done. He was torn between killing her or fucking her. He wanted to feel her tight insides, but he also wanted to strangle her to death, and seeing her only made that clear.

Trisha jumped into his arms, wrapping her arms and legs around him like a spider monkey. She had missed him so much, and now she was going to be with him, at least in this moment she was. She didn't care if it only lasted for tonight or if it lasted forever. The simple fact she was going to be with him was perfect.

He took in her scent, missing the way she smelled and the way her body felt.

"I missed you, Dutch. I'm so, so sorry," she said as she slid off of him and dropped to the ground. Her favorite thing to do was suck his dick while he held her hair and forced her head down on his dick. She didn't want it soft tonight; she wanted it rough like it always was.

"What are you sorry for?"

Dutch unzipped his pants and pulled his long and fat dick out of his pants, his veins throbbing with murder.

"I'm sorry for r-r—"

She was silenced by Dutch sliding his dick in her

mouth and pushing it all the way back to the end of her throat.

"I can't hear you. Sorry for what?"

"R-r—"

Trisha's stomach turned as she almost threw up from how far he was pushing his dick down her throat.

"Robbing you. I'm sorry for stealing from you."

"Mhmm…show me how sorry you are."

Trisha began pulling out her best dick sucking moves. She was sucking his dick like it was the last dick she would ever suck in her life.

"Little girl, what did you do with my gold?"

Dutch had been wondering that for the last few weeks, but his mind had been preoccupied on thoughts of Junie, wondering if she was back with Wild Bill or not.

But now, he needed to know. If he could get them back, he would have them. If not, he would definitely be getting revenge, starting here tonight.

"Cocaine has them, but I can get them back," Trisha said as saliva spilled from her mouth.

Dutch was about to cum. He could never hold it in too long when Trisha was giving it to him, but he knew that she couldn't get his golden bricks back. They were gone now that they were in the hands of Cocaine, so Trisha was no longer useful, and he hated to do it to her, but he would let his seed spill down her throat one last time before it was all said and done.

Dutch grabbed the back of her head and began fucking her mouth viciously. He was ready to nut, and the thought of killing her only made his nut bubble up faster.

As soon as he shot his warm, thick cum down her throat, she looked him in the eyes, and smiled with his dick still in her mouth.

There was nothing left for Dutch to say. He didn't need to say another word because no matter what he said, it wasn't going to change what he was about to do.

Dutch reached behind him with one hand and rubbed her face with the other. Slowly, he moved his arm in front of him, and without a pause or any hesitation at all, he retrieved his gun and then pulled the trigger and shot Trisha dead in the face.

When he pulled away from her, her eyes were wide open, and she was looking directly up at him. She still had love in her eyes. The horror of being shot never reached her mind.

Dutch didn't want her necessarily to suffer, but she did have to pay for her disobedience and disloyalty, and unfortunately, that price was her life.

Surgery for Wild Bill was a piece of cake. He would have literally done anything for Lexxy, anything to see her be happy, and of course, anything to keep her alive. He had already been a great father to her whether any of them knew it or not. He was doing things for her like a father would do before he gave up his kidney. To him, it was a small thing so his little girl could be healthy and have what she needed.

Wild Bill had always wished Lexxy was his daughter, and strangely enough, his dream just happened to come true. It had always been true; he just didn't know it himself.

He remembered when Lexxy was growing up, she'd always complained about not being able to really know Dutch's family or Junie's family, but that was because their families were trash. Dutch's family loved him dearly, but he did his best to stay away from them to keep them safe, but he still had full records of his family, where they came from, and pictures that he wanted to show Lexxy. He wanted her to see where his family line started, and today was the first day he'd be seeing her since even before the surgery.

Though Wild Bill felt fear in his heart, for the most

part, he just wanted to get it out of the way and get it over with. He wanted the awkwardness he was feeling in his gut to be gone so he could enjoy knowing that Lexxy was his daughter. He didn't call her out of fear of her not answering, and she hadn't reached out to him either. He figured she was still just as surprised as he was, but he wanted to reassure her that he didn't know. He had no idea that she was his daughter because if he did, he would've said something before now, and he would've been acting accordingly, but that wasn't possible because he truly didn't know. He also wanted to make sure Lexxy wasn't giving her mother a hard time because of the secret she kept.

Wild Bill had never driven so slow in his life. The closer he got to the house, he wanted to talk himself out of what he was doing, but he wasn't going to do that. He needed to talk to her, even if it made him extremely uncomfortable and sick to the stomach. Normally, he would drink the feelings away, but he couldn't do that. This was his Lexxy he was thinking about and being drunk would only ruin the moment that he was trying to create, not to mention, he'd just given up a kidney. Drinking was definitely against the doctor's orders, for now.

With sweaty palms, Wild Bill pulled up in front of Cocaine and Lexxy's house and thought about how he would lead, or what he should start by saying, and he figured there was nothing better than the truth of course.

He rung the doorbell, and through the glass, colored window pangs, he could see her bouncy-self making her way to the door. He hadn't seen her move like that in a very long time, and he was just thankful that he had something to do with how well she was able to get around.. He loved seeing her up on her feet like this. It just wasn't going to get any better than what it was right now.

Lexxy opened the door, and she was stopped dead in her tracks. She couldn't move; she was stuck in her spot. Though Wild Bill was afraid, Lexxy was overjoyed to see her father standing in her doorway.

"Would you like to come in?" she asked as she moved out of the way with her hand open, gesturing for him to come inside.

"Yes, please."

The sweat from Wild Bill's hands were imprinted on the folder with the pictures he wanted to show Lexxy, but he still planned to show them to her even if they did appear messed up. Some of the pictures were in black and white, and that was where it all began; Wild Bill's line of people.

"What are you doing here?" she asked curiously.

"Damn, your pops ain't welcome here?" he said half-jokingly.

"Of course. You know you're always welcome here. I just thought I was never going to see you again, per your words, not mine."

"Yeah, that was until your mama dropped that loud ass bomb on us. I would never abandon my kid, never. I may not have been your father, or a father figure, but I was always in your life, and I did my best to be around you as much as possible. That was just when I thought you were my niece. I wish I would have known, Lexxy. I'm sorry, baby. I'm so sorry."

"I'm not mad at you or Mama. I just want to know why y'all didn't tell me that you all had been together in the past. Why keep that a secret from me?"

"I didn't want to tell you because that shit seemed irrelevant. I have never stopped loving your mama, and I thought when I got out, she was going to come back home with me, but she got pregnant with you, with the baby that I thought was Dutch's at the time, but apparently not. I don't know. I also didn't want to tell you because I didn't want you thinkin' differently of your mama. You're not judge-mental, but baby girl, you got the tendency to think shit is supposed to be a certain way, and when it ain't that way, you act a little funny."

Lexxy wanted to be mad, but she knew he was telling the truth. Wild Bill was right; Lexxy always had preconceived notions about people whether they came from her or the people, and she believed in keeping those intact at all costs, and finding something like this out at an earlier date may have fucked her up.

"Anyway, I came over here because I want you to see where you come from, where you really come from."

Wild Bill walked over to the couch with Lexxy, and he opened his folder up and began taking the pictures out showing her who her extended family was.

"This is your Grandma Pearl. She's actually still alive."

"Your mom? Your mom is alive? Why haven't I ever met her?"

"I stayed away to keep her safe, and Mama wasn't havin' none of that street mess, so I kept it movin'."

Wild Bill sat there with Lexxy, catching her up on all that she'd missed and didn't know. He wanted her to be a part of his life as much as she could be at this point. He wanted her to know all she could know, and although they had nothing but time, especially now that she had the kidney, he didn't want this day to end, and he was afraid that as soon as he stopped talking, the day would somehow be over.

Cocaine and Junie watched from the upstairs banister as the two laughed and hugged one another, spending time together, and enjoying themselves.

Cocaine was happy that Lexxy was able to learn about her heritage, and that they were learning so much from one another. Junie realized all that she had robbed her daughter of, and that pang of guilt washed over her once more. She loved her daughter and wanted her to be able to experience a full life with family, no matter what part of the family that was.

As Cocaine watched Lexxy with Wild Bill, he began thinking about his grandmother and how he'd gone to Texas to get her ring and how he really didn't know his grandmother, but that he might like to change that. Lexxy was figuring out where she came from, and even though Cocaine knew where and who he came from, he still wanted to be around family. Besides that, he hadn't visited his mother's grave in years, and he wanted to take Lexxy there. Once she got done with Wild Bill, Cocaine was going to talk to her about going to Texas for a little road trip. They were family now, and if they ever did have kids, it was important for everyone to know where their children's bloodlines origins were really from.

CHAPTER 13

Cocaine left Wild Bill and Lexxy to talk on their own. He kept feeling like he was an intruder in something that didn't have shit to do with him anyway, and he knew that Lexxy would tell him about it later. He wanted to make sure she had her privacy so she could have her moment alone, and her time with her father, who even though he had been in her life, he was now finally able to step into the father role.

Cocaine had to go and get the gold that Trisha dropped off; more like he had to go outside to get it, but he figured he would stay outside in case there was something inside the bag that didn't need to be seen.

A black town Lincoln pulled up, and Cocaine simply went to the car, pulled the bag out of the back, and hit the car on the top three times with his fist once he was done. He didn't need to say a word; this was one of his personal drivers, he already knew what to do.

Cocaine sat on the front porch of his home, where he knew there was no view from the street, and he began going through the bag. All of the gold was ridiculous. He couldn't understand why his father would leave so much of this behind and why he wouldn't have just gone and got the gold cashed in for money. That was what Cocaine would have done. As he went through the bag though, he noticed something strange—a few of the golden blocks weren't as shiny as the others. Some of them damn near blinded him, and then, there were a few that didn't seem like they had that shine to them, like they had been dulled, or even like they were fake.

Cocaine went through the bag in its entirety, pulling each golden brick out, examining it. Separating it. If it shined, it could stay in the bag, if it didn't, it had to come out.

By the time he went through the bag, he found at least ten of the golden bricks that didn't seem right. He held them up to his face, and on the side of one of them, there was something white coming out of it like a piece of paper. He pulled on it, and pulled on it, and finally, the golden brick opened up, and there was a piece of paper inside.

"What the fuck is this?" Cocaine asked himself aloud. He had no idea what any of this could mean.

He unrolled the paper that was carefully rolled into a cylinder, pulled it open, and began reading.

To my dear baby boy, Cocaine,

You're not even here yet, but I can feel you moving inside of me. I can't wait to meet your little face. I started this journal so that one day, you'd have these to look back on, and know exactly how I felt at the time I was carrying you. I love you so, so very much.

He had never seen his mother's handwriting before, nor had he ever known anything she'd ever said about him or to him, not really. Whenever he brought his mother up to his father, he acted as if he had nothing to say, so Cocaine never pressed the issue, no matter how hard he wanted to, but he hoped there would be something for him to look forward to in all of these golden bricks, or at least the ones that pulled apart.

Coco, now listen, your father is going to try and take credit for giving you that nickname, but it's actually mine. I came up with the name. We got more pictures of you today, and you are going to be a big boy. Your hands were so big and your feet, your father said he already knew you were a boy before they even told us. He's a liar, and honestly, he claims he wanted a boy, but his face looked so upset when the nurse said that we were having you. Either way, I'm just glad you're happy and you're healthy. I love you, baby boy.

Cocaine went on to read more notes, and the more he read, the closer he felt to his mother, and he could now understand why his father kept these notes in the fake golden bricks, so that one day, he'd be able to have a fortune, but of course, he'd find a part of his mother that he was never able to know when she was alive.

Though Cocaine had already decided, he was definitely taking Lexxy to Texas. He really had to go and visit his mother's grave now, and he was going to go as soon as possible. When Cocaine walked back in the house, he didn't see Wild Bill anymore, and he wondered how he was able to miss him leaving the house.

"Bae, where's Bill?"

"Up there talkin' to Mama. I told them I would give them some privacy," Lexxy said, rolling her eyes.

"You sure that's a good idea? I mean, the last time they were probably alone, you were conceived. I'm just sayin'?"

"Shut up, baby. What's that in your hand?" Lexxy noticed the all-black duffle bag that he carried, almost like a baby in the house.

"Well, you already know what I was doin' at Dutch's house that day, and this bag is full of gold and stuff from my mother. I had already said I was gon' do this, and I really want to now before the wedding, but I wanna take you to Texas and let you meet my people, well, whatever people I have left. Seein' you with Bill stirred up some feelings, and I need to go visit my mother's gravesite. I ain't been in so fuckin' long."

"When are we going?" Lexxy was very excited. She had been dying to see where Cocaine grew up. He'd been all over her stomping grounds, but now, it was time for him to show her around, and she couldn't wait.

"We can go whenever you want, baby. I'm 'bout to start lookin' up flights now. We can probably leave tomorrow, go ahead and start packing."

Cocaine didn't have to tell her twice. She was out of here in the blink of an eye. She couldn't wait to get to Texas. Ever since Cocaine had given her his grandmother's ring, she had been dying to meet the grandmother and thank her because now she felt like she was a part of the family. That ring held more importance and value than either of them could truly ever know though.

Cocaine sat the bag down and plopped on the couch and started looking up the flights. They could actually leave as early as that night if they hurried up. There was a flight leaving out at nine p.m, and it was only five. Cocaine could be packed and ready, but he didn't know if Lexxy could.

"Baby, can you be ready to go in an hour?"

"An hour? Oh, Lord, yeah, I'm just not gonna be able to shower."

"Why you need a shower anyway? You been in here gettin' dirty? The only dirt you better have comin' off ya' body is the dirt I put there. Hurry up, girl. Our flight leaves at nine."

Suddenly, Cocaine heard her little feet pattering around the room, moving in lightning speed. Lexxy had been known to take a long time to do everything, literally, whether it was pack or eat, she would take a long time doing some shit, but he needed her to move quick today so they would be on time to the airport. Going through security could be a bitch, and he didn't have time for that.

Cocaine carried the bag with him into the bedroom. He knew he shouldn't bring it with him, but he did want the notes inside, so he cracked open the remaining bricks and took the notes out and put them in his wallet. He wanted to carry them with him always, and eventually, he'd have to get something more than a wallet to carry them in.

Six hours later….

Lexxy was able to get done packing in record time, they made it to the airport and didn't miss their flight, and they landed safely in H-Town around eleven-thirty.

Though it was nighttime, and it was almost midnight, Houston was a place that never slept. It was still so lively, and there were so many people moving around, even outside of the airport.

"So, what hotel are we staying in?"

"We ain't stayin' in no hotel, baby, we 'bout to hit up my Grandmama's house."

Lexxy was surprised by this. A woman Cocaine had only met once, he was now feeling her enough to go stay in her home, but she was just happy that he was able to still have a living relative and have something to reach out to, to come back home to.

Cocaine called a Lyft for them; he said Taxis were too old school, and they were too young to be ridin' around in a yellow ass car. The Lyft driver pulled up two minutes after he was called, and to Lexxy's surprise, he was a great tour guide, and he knew so many things about the city. As they drove around, getting closer to Cocaine's grandmother's house, he was pointing out certain sites and attractions, and things for them to check out while they were there on their stay. Lexxy was already falling in love with Houston. It was truly a beautiful place

The ride from the airport to Cocaine's grandmother's house was about thirty minutes, but it was so full of information, Lexxy didn't even mind. It was wonderful. When they got to the house, Lexxy realized no one other than a grandmother could live in this house. It was very quaint, and the front yard looked like the lord himself had come down and touched it. It was organized, colorful, and overall just beautiful.

"You ready?" Cocaine asked Lexxy as he bent down and kissed her on the mouth.

"Uhn-uhn, now, boy, don't be gettin' all fresh in front of my house. Bring y'all behinds on here 'for you catch cold, ya' hear me?"

· Cocaine's grandmother emerged from what seemed like nowhere. Had she been watching them this whole entire time? He didn't know. He never had anyone to call him out on his shit either, so this was very interesting for him to see, but he wouldn't disrespect his grandmother. He was a guest in her home, and he wouldn't dare do anything to displease her.

When they got into the house, Cocaine greeted his grandmother, and then he went straight into introducing Lexxy.

"Grandmama, this is Lexxy, Lexxy, this is my grandmother, Ella Mae."

"Oh, you can call me whatever you want. Y'all hungry? I didn't know if you would be, but I went ahead and cooked anyway. You can never have enough food."

"I am starved! What do you have for us, Grandmama?" Lexxy was fitting right in. She didn't stumble, nor did the words seem strange coming out of her mouth.

"You look like you could use a good meal, come on in hea, gal."

Lexxy followed closely behind her; she didn't want to miss a second of the food that was about to be given out.

When they entered the kitchen, there was so much

food on the table, Lexxy just prayed her stomach was as big as her eyes were right now. She wanted to inhale the whole table.

"Baby, pace yourself. Remember, you've been looking at wedding dresses, and I don't give a fuck how big you get, but you gon' care when you can't fit into one that you really like."

"Fuck it. If I get fat, I get fat. I'm about to grub."

When Lexxy was sick, there were certain foods she wasn't allowed to have anymore, mainly fried foods, and since she had her kidney transplant, and it was a success, she'd been inhaling pounds of food. Cocaine didn't give a damn if she got big, he just knew she would be miserable if she couldn't fit into the wedding gown that she was eyeing. He knew she would never forgive herself, so he tried to keep giving her little reminders here and there about it for her own sake, but if she didn't care, he didn't either.

"A wedding? Oh, that's right, let me see my ring, chile. Let me see what it looks like on your hand."

Lexxy held her hand out as she took a seat at the table. Ella Mae was very happy to see her ring again, and even happier that she was going to be able to keep it in the family.

"So, when is the wedding?"

"Yeah, Lexxy, when is the wedding?" Cocaine asked, sarcastically.

"We haven't set a date yet."

Lexxy wasn't being short because she didn't want to talk about it, she just wanted to eat. She felt like she was starving, and she wanted to consume the whole house if she could.

"No date? Uhn-uhn, we gon' fix all that tonight, baby. I'm an old woman, but I can still make some plans. Wait, I am invited, right?" Ella Mae asked with a sincere look in her eyes.

Cocaine rose from the seat he'd just sat down in, got up and went to his grandmother's side, and kissed her on the side of her chubby jaw. "Of course, you are. Ain't no weddin' without the one who started the line, Grandmama. Come on now!"

Ella Mae smiled. She was going to stay up all night with them so they could get this wedding together. She could see the love the two of them shared just from the way they interacted, and she was thankful to have Lexxy become part of her family and carry on the Blackwood name.

The next morning, though they had been up for most of the night, Cocaine couldn't sleep anymore. For some reason, he felt a sense of urgency to get to his mother's gravesite. He looked over and saw that Lexxy was still asleep, and he didn't want to interrupt her, so he figured he'd go by himself. They'd literally only had three hours of sleep, but his heart wasn't at rest. He had to get out of the house.

His grandmother the night before had laid out her car keys and told him if he had somewhere to go, he could use the keys, which right now, he was grateful for because he didn't want to have to wait on a Lyft to get him around town.

He jumped into the car and realized his grandmother had style and that she must've had a little money stashed away since she was driving a Lexus, but he didn't have time to be thinking about that. He pulled off and headed to the cemetery.

When he got there, his mind was cloudy. Something was disturbing his heart, and he just didn't know what it was. He hoped something bad wasn't about to happen to Lexxy or to him, or to his grandmother even. Now he felt stupid for even leaving the house. His emotions were up and down and all over the damn place.

He parked his car near the information center that was also built like a tiny house. It had been years since Cocaine came to his mother's gravesite, and he couldn't remember exactly where it was, but he was sure he would find it.

As he walked around, he saw several people with the last name Blackwood written on their headstones, which in a way, frightened Cocaine. He didn't want to end up like all of these people, dead because of a beef that was old and that nobody would let go of. He didn't want that for himself, nor for his beautiful soon to be bride, but he valued legacy and family above all, so he felt torn.

After wandering around for some time, he finally stumbled upon the grave. He could see her large headstone sticking out of the ground. He went toward it, with his eyes steady on the headstone, reading it to himself. ***"What could have been, wasn't nearly long enough."***

If that wasn't the truth. There was still so much he didn't know about his mother, and he just didn't know if he'd ever be able to find out at this rate. Who could he go to, to talk about his mother? Sure, he'd found her letters, but the letters were nothing in comparison to actually having her or having someone who was close to her to inform him.

The closer Cocaine got, the more he realized, something wasn't right. In front of her grave, it seemed to be sunken in, and he wondered if it was just from the rain, or where it was coming from.

Cocaine was now running full speed, trying to figure out what the fuck was going on with his mother's gravesite, and when he got there, his heart shattered. It literally fell out of his mouth, onto the ground, and exploded.

The ground was empty. There was no casket, no body, no nothing.

"Where the hell could she be?" he asked aloud, wondering where a dead body could disappear to. This couldn't be right. This was definitely her headstone. It had her name and the quote his father had came up with himself. Where the fuck was his mother?

Cocaine took off running back toward the information center and burst in the door, ready to fuck some shit up.

"Yo', what's goin' on with my mother's grave? Jayla Barnett?"

Juaqeen and Cocaine's mother weren't married, at least not legally, but according to the streets, they were.

The office attendant didn't even have to look up. He knew exactly whose grave that was, and he'd been paid to keep quiet, so he would do so.

"Sir, I'm sorry to have to tell you this, but we've had the worst time keeping grave robbers away from here. Whatever was inside of her casket must have been valuable since they've taken the whole thing, casket and all. I'm sorry, but we did file a police report."

"Fuck a report, why wasn't someone notified? Why wasn't I called?"

Then Cocaine remembered that he was a baby when his mother died, and his father was obviously still alive and thought he was going to live forever. Cocaine never thought to come and change the information at the gravesite. He never thought that anything like this would happen.

That bad feeling in his stomach was clearly leading him to this moment; he just wished he knew what the fuck was going on.

After finding out about the police report, going to the police station and reading it himself, some shit sounded fishy. It just didn't seem right that someone would choose his mother's graves out of all the fucking graves in there unless he was being targeted for something. He didn't know what that could be, but he did have enemies everywhere, so it could have been anyone.

Cocaine had been gone most of the morning, and Lexxy was blowing his phone up once he sent her a picture of the grave his mother was supposed to be in. When he got back to his grandmother's house, she was making breakfast.

Cocaine burst through the door, anger dripping and reeking from his body like a disease.

"Cocaine, get yo' behind in here. Don't come in this house and not speak."

Cocaine was in his own world, and he was on his way up the stairs, but when he heard his grandmother's voice, he remembered he wasn't by himself, and this was no time to fall apart or act out. His grandmother was kind enough to let them stay in her home, and he wanted to make sure he gave her the utmost respect. Besides that, she'd helped them plan their entire wedding overnight. The venue was still in the air simply because they hadn't called and checked yet, but that was what Lexxy had planned to do this morning, after she went to the gravesite with Cocaine, but that clearly didn't and wasn't going to happen now.

"I'm sorry, Grandmama. How you doin' this mornin'?"

"Well, baby, I was doin' pretty good 'til I saw that picture that Lexxy showed me. I'm so sorry, baby."

"You? Shit, me too, but that's ok, 'cuz I already know how this 'bout to play out."

Lexxy looked over at Cocaine, and all she saw was red. She could see the blood pumping and rushing through his body ready to spill out and ruin all things good.

"Watch your mouth, boy. Wooh, you remind me of

your father, mad as all hell and don't give a damn what's goin' on around him. Now listen to what I'm 'bout to tell ya', 'cuz you ain't gon' like it. You're about to get married to a beautiful chocolate woman; you ain't got no damn time to be worryin' 'bout who did this, ya' hear? I ain't tellin' ya' to let it go, I'm tellin' ya' to let it go for now. The year y'all done had, you just gettin' each other back. Don't do nothin' stupid to ruin the time y'all got together. Besides, the best revenge is a silent one."

Ella Mae tilted her spatula at Cocaine and turned back around to the stove.

It was strange, but she was right. Revenge was best served when it was unknown, but that didn't ease the pain of him not knowing who would do something like this to him?

"Besides, we got a wedding to go to soon, and we need to make sure you show up for your own weddin', ain't that right, Lexxy?"

"That's right, Grandmama."

Cocaine sat down beside Lexxy and held her hand. She didn't need to say anything to him. He knew what she was thinking and how she was feeling. Besides that, when you shared the kind of love they did, words weren't shit anyway. It was all about feeling, about emotion, it was all about what was inside.

After breakfast, Lexxy and Cocaine headed upstairs. At first, Lexxy wanted to fuck Cocaine's brains out. She loved when he got all strong and crazy, and all angry like the Hulk, but not right now. She just wanted to hold her man. Cocaine had pretty much only cried over Lexxy and his father, but he was about to shed a few tears for his mother too.

They climbed into bed, and Lexxy reached for Cocaine to lie back on her. She opened her arms, and like a baby, Cocaine wrapped his arms around her small mid-section, locking his fingers around her, and he cried. His heart was so full of pain, and it was pouring out onto Lexxy's stomach. He wept not only for what had happened, but for what was coming, and he didn't know what was going on or who he could trust, but he damn sure wasn't about to leave his grandmama here when somebody could be out lurking, fucking some shit up. He wouldn't do that to her.

"Let's go home, today. We can exchange our tickets, and I'ma get Grandmama one, and we gon' be out of here."

Lexxy was sad to hear that because she was having a great time and really wanted to see more of Texas, but she also understood what was going on, and she didn't want to further upset him.

Cocaine slid off the bed and he went back downstairs to talk his grandmother into going with them, but there was no talk necessary.

"These walls are thin, baby. I hear everything. You ain't got to beg me to come. If you think I'll be safer with you, then I'll go. That way, I can really help get some shit done for the wedding. I'll pack a bag."

"Nah, Grandmama, you don't need none of this stuff, none of it. We can buy you all new stuff."

"You that ready to go?"

"Yeah, we need to get out the city."

Cocaine was right, because what he didn't know was, there was a presence lurking around his grandmother's house, but the hairs on the back of his neck were standing up, alerting him to the danger that was near them. He had to get out of that house, and it had to be now.

Three months later, there were still no leads on who had dug up Cocaine's mother's body, but he tried not to think about it too much. He and Lexxy's wedding was in just another week or so, and that was his main priority. His grandmother had been a tremendous help, and she got along with Junie and Wild Bill so well. This was what he always wanted, a family that could get along together and coexist in general happiness.

Everywhere Cocaine and Lexxy went, she was snapping pictures of them with the hashtag #Blackwoodwedding with the count-down of the wedding next to it, and she would post it on every social media site she owned.

This somewhat concerned Cocaine because he worried about what would happen if the enemy, whoever that was, saw their happiness and came after Lexxy? He couldn't fight the sickness in her body before, but if somebody came after his baby, he would literally lose his own life protecting hers, and Cocaine wasn't nothin' to play with, but he wouldn't ruin Lexxy's excitement, not for one minute.

In the middle of them snapping pictures, Lexxy's

phone began ringing, and the name Dutch appeared boldly with emojis plastered around it.

"Hold up," Lexxy said as she stepped away to take the phone call.

"Hello?"

"Hey, Lexxy. I saw you called me."

It was true, Lexxy had been calling Dutch because she wanted to talk to him. At the end of the day, this was her wedding, and she wanted him to be a part of it no matter what.

"Yeah, well, how are you doing? Took you long enough to call me back."

Dutch was silent. He didn't want to say the wrong thing. He loved Lexxy, but her being Wild Bill's daughter was almost too much for his heart to take.

"I'm good, what's up?"

"Well, I just…I wanted to invite you to the wedding. I know how you're feeling about Mom and Wild Bill right now, but you're still my father too. You raised me and taught me most of the things I know. I can't imagine getting married and you not being there."

Dutch didn't know what to say. He wanted to say to count him in, that he would be there, but he didn't know if that was entirely true. Plus, he wanted to know if he was walking her down the aisle, or just attending.

"Well, is Bill walking you down the aisle? Are you asking me as a back up?"

"Woah, you're not a back up. You never have been, nor will you ever be. You should know that by now. I love you just as much as I love him. I did ask him to walk me down the aisle only because I thought you were going to say no, but I still want you to be——"

"Say less. I'll be there. Just send me the details, and I'll show up. Y'all registered anywhere?"

Lexxy knew Dutch's feelings were hurt, but with the way he'd been acting, how else were things going to go? He had been acting like a brat this entire time. He didn't want to answer her phone calls or any of that, so what else could he expect? She had shit to do, names to put claims to, and she didn't have time to be waiting on him to answer her.

"Yeah, I'll send you the list, but you don't have to get us a gift; your presence is more than enough."

"Cool. I'll be there, Lexxy. Just know that I love you. I always have, and I always will, but this has been hard on me. I feel like ain't nobody takin' my feelings into account."

"That's not true. I am, or at least I'm trying to. Listen, after I get back from my honeymoon, we can spend a lot of time together. I mean, a lot of time just catching up and trying to mend the fences, what do you say?"

Dutch had no choice but to agree. He didn't want to be estranged from his daughter, but Wild Bill still had to pay for what he did, and if he had to get him at the wedding, since he hadn't been able to find him, that was what it was going to have to be. He only hoped Lexxy would forgive him for what he was about to do.

"That's fine with me, baby girl. Look, I gotta go. You enjoy your day, and congratulations again. I love you."

"I love you too, Daddy."

Hearing Lexxy call him daddy made a lump swell up in his throat, but he ended the call strong and went on about his day.

Lexxy had walked away a little bit from Cocaine

because she knew how her talking to Dutch made him feel, but when she came back, he had a smile plastered across his face.

"What's all that about?" Lexxy asked swirling her fingers around, gesturing to his smile.

"I know you wanted him to come, and by the look on your face, I guess he's coming."

"He is. I know you hate him, and hell, I hate his ass too sometimes, but the man raised me, and I want him to be there."

"I ain't gon' argue with you, baby. If that's what the queen wants, that's what the queen shall have."

Cocaine was being extra with her, but she thought it was cute. He got down on his knee and kissed her ring like she was the pope.

"Stop it, boy! Get up. Come on, we got more pictures to take."

Any other time, Cocaine would complain about pictures, but after finding those letters from his mother, he realized how important memories were, and he wanted to create as many as he could with Lexxy, especially before the fall out that was approaching, and it was coming soon.

Lucky was scrolling through his Instagram, double tapping pictures of everyone he knew, even if he didn't like the picture really, but he knew each like counted.

As he continued scrolling, he came across Lexxy's

pictures. She was a trending topic. In bold letters, of all the pictures, the only word he noticed was **Wedding**. He knew eventually Lexxy and Cocaine were getting married, but the fact that it was happening this soon gave him some pause and brought about heart ache. How could she be ready to settle down with Cocaine so quickly? Did what they had previously mean nothing to her? How was she over it already?

Meanwhile, Lucky was sitting at home looking like a lost puppy, sad that he'd lost his favorite chew toy. He lost his woman, officially. He knew this day would come, and when it did, he would do everything he could to win her back. This was going to be his last attempt. He would be at her wedding, since she was posting exactly where it would be and the time, and even if he had to steal her away, she was going to be his once more.

He would leave Carley's ass alone, and go back home with Lexxy, or if they had to create a new home, he would do that too. He just wanted to be back with her. He messed up in ways he could never truly fix, but he was willing to try if he was just given the shot.

Lexxy, Zeke, and Lucky could all be a family, if she was just willing to give it a chance.

Lexxy and Cocaine opted out of a bachelor and bachelorette party. They just wanted to spend the time they had together, together.

Denise wanted strippers, but Lexxy made it clear that she wouldn't be partaking in any of those festivities, so Denise decided to throw her a bachelorette party for herself, and she had a good time.

The next morning, when Denise showed up to the wedding, she had alcohol pouring out of her system, but she was on time, and she was there; that was all Lexxy actually cared about.

"Denise, come on, we gotta get ready."

Denise was moving slow, but she had it together. She was on the move, just not as quickly as Lexxy would've liked, but she didn't care. If she had to put on her make-up, dress, and shoes by herself, then she would.

As Lexxy and Denise were getting ready, a knock came at the door. Luckily, she still had on her robe. When she went to the door, Wild Bill was standing there with a smile on his face.

"My bad, I guess this is the wrong room."

"You know it is. What are you doing here?"

Wild Bill flashed back to when Lexxy had asked him

to walk her down the aisle, and of course, he said yes. This was a moment he never thought he'd have. Even now that she knew that he was her father, he still thought she'd ask Dutch, but she didn't. She asked him, and that was the greatest honor in all the world.

"I just wanted to see you, I wanted to see you one last time as my little girl."

"I'll always be your little girl. Now go get ready, sometimes you take longer than me."

Lexxy reached up and kissed Wild Bill on the cheek, and then she closed the door.

This day was going to be epic, and she couldn't wait to be Mrs. Blackwood.

Cocaine stood in the mirror looking at himself. He was handsome and he knew it. Ella Mae was in there with him, assisting him with his bow tie and his overall suit. She was so proud of him. She'd always wished that Juaqeen would've gotten married so she would have had this joy by now, but he didn't. His life was cut down and cut short before it could even happen.

"You look good, grandson."

"Thank you, you're not looking too shabby yourself."

Ella Mae was dressed in a cream dress with a hat to match. She was from the old school, and you wore hats to weddings. She knew she looked good too, hell she started the bloodline of looking good.

"I'm proud of you, Cocaine. I haven't known you

long, but in the time I have, I've seen the man you've become and the man you're becoming, and it's a sight to see. Your father would be proud of you."

Cocaine had waited his whole life to hear those words. He always wished they would have come directly from his father, but hearing them from his grandmother wasn't too bad either.

"Thank you. Come on, let me get you down to your seat so I can go out here and wait for my bride."

"Baby, the weddin' don't start for another hour. You gon' wait for an hour?"

"I've waited a lifetime for this type of happiness, what's an hour?"

"Ok."

Ella Mae couldn't argue with that. She was just happy to be there in the moment and to be able to help Cocaine in his moment of greatness.

Cocaine grabbed Ella Mae's hand and walked her down to the front row. On the way down, he greeted the people who were already sitting down. Some of them he recognized, others he didn't. Most of these people were people Lexxy knew. He'd invited a few people from back home, but not many. Most of them were just for security, but they blended in with the crowd well.

He was on his way to happiness, and he couldn't wait. He just knew Lexxy was going to be beautiful in her wedding gown, and he hoped the photographer they hired would do a good job of capturing their special moment. He wanted to be able to show these to their children when they got older, whenever they had them really. He was proud to be marrying Lexxy, and nothing and no one could stand in their way as long as they were together.

Wild Bill was in his room, admiring the venue Lexxy had chosen to get married in. It was a large church. Though he wasn't expecting that, he figured it was Ella Mae's doing, but the church was huge, and it was historic. It was a mega church, and the pastor had agreed to wed them though they weren't members of the church. Money went a long way, and Wild Bill could only imagine what his portion of the money he gave Lexxy for the wedding was going to.

Wild Bill sat in his room, half dressed, almost getting drunk, but he knew that was inappropriate, so he tried to slow himself down. He figured it would be best if he pissed most of it out, so he went to the bathroom that was attached to his room and began peeing.

It was one of the greatest pees he'd ever taken, but it could have been the last pee he was ever going to take.

While he was flushing the toilet, he thought he heard something, but the toilet was loud, so he wasn't sure. He peaked his head out, and though he didn't see anyone, he knew what he heard, so he came out of the bathroom after washing his hands and sitting at the table he was just about to fall pray to drunkenness at, Dutch sat.

"Who in the hell let yo' ass in here?"

"You ain't hard to find. I just followed the scent of alcohol."

"Yeah, ok!" Wild Bill said. He wasn't afraid. He knew this day was going to come, and that was why he always kept some kind of weapon on him; a knife, a gun, switch blade, something.

"See, now I know I'ma just have to kill you. I done let you slide for too long," Dutch said as he sipped Bourbon from the crystal embossed glass.

"Well then, come on, nigga. I was tryna do Lexxy a favor; it ain't even about you. I was a good friend to you, a loyal worker, but you ain't trustworthy, bitch! But today ain't the day, now excuse me while I go walk MY daughter down the aisle." Wild Bill couldn't believe Dutch was going this far, especially in here. This was too much, but if this was how it had to be, it would be that way.

When Dutch didn't rush him, or even move, he figured Dutch didn't want any smoke, so he was ready to go on and get outside. Looking at the clock on the wall, it was almost time for him to meet Lexxy, and he didn't want to be late or disappoint her. He'd already wasted too much time drinking and on Dutch.

Wild Bill pulled his tuxedo jacket closed and headed for the door when all of a sudden, he felt something hard and sharp hit the back of his head. It made him stumble forward, and he hit his forehead on the table that sat next to the door.

Blood gushed everywhere, and Dutch was pleased. Wild Bill had him fucked up if he thought he was goin' watch him walk Lexxy, the child HE raised walk down the aisle with him on his arm. Fuck him, and if he bled to death on the floor of the church, they'd all be better off for it, at least that's what Dutch thought.

The melodious sounds of Lisa Tucker's "I Am For You" played throughout the church, igniting love and passion inside of all the guests. Lexxy was waiting behind the double doors as the intro played to her wedding song. This was the moment she'd been waiting for. After all the crazy shit, the heartbreak, the hospital visits, transplant fail and all, she was here, with her man, and she was finally going to be his.

With her bouquet tucked tightly in her hand, she peaked around both corners, looking for Wild Bill, but she didn't see him. She hated to leave her spot, but what choice did she have? She had to do something.

She remembered where he was getting ready and went to find him. She wouldn't be surprised if he was somewhere passed out drunk. Lexxy wouldn't even be mad about that because she knew him, and she knew how he got when he was nervous. Some called it social anxiety; Lexxy called it alcoholism.

She went to the door and prepared to knock, when someone reached for her shoulder.

Lexxy turned around with a smile on her face, assuming it was Wild Bill. She moved her hand-beaded, ivory train out of the way and pushed her matching veil to the side as it had fallen in her face. When she looked up, she was surprised and worried about the hazel eyes she was looking into.

"Lu-Lucky, what are you doing here?"

Lucky had eased his way past everyone without even being seen. He was dressed like he was a guest at the wedding, and no one bothered to ask him if he was invited. He played the part. He'd seen their wedding colors on Instagram, so he could be what he needed to be to get in. This was his last hope of getting with Lexxy, and he had to take it now.

"I came to get you, baby. Come on, we can leave now and live happily ever after."

"Oh, God. Happily ever after? Are you fucking kidding me? Lucky, leave me the fuck alone!"

"No, I tried that, and it didn't work. We were happy once; we could be happy again."

"We can never be happy again. You ruined us, and I've moved the fuck on! I thought you had too, what is your problem?"

Lexxy tried moving away from him, but he had her cornered. Lucky was always a lot stronger than her, but she hoped if she tried to step away that he wouldn't get in her way. She tried to step aside, but he just stepped in front of her. She tried the same move again going toward the opposite way, but he did it again.

"Lucky, move, I'm not playin' with you!"

"And neither am I!"

A chilling voice came out of nowhere, stopping them both dead in their tracks. Lexxy knew this voice, but she couldn't figure out where she heard it.

Lexxy looked over Lucky's shoulder, and there Carley stood with her gun pointed at the both of them.

"I told yo' stupid ass to stop testing me. I knew I couldn't trust you. I knew I couldn't. I've been watching you the last couple of days, getting ready for this wedding. You think I didn't notice? Nah, I just didn't say anything. I wanted to see if you would actually go through with it, and you did, and the funny part is, you were setting things up perfectly for me."

Lucky couldn't believe Carley was pulling this shit, and she looked a mess.

"Carley, where's Zeke?"

"Don't worry about ya' son now, nigga, you wasn't worried when you were messin' around with this hoe, and yo' ass just won't die, will you? Unplugging machines and shit, and you still don't know how to stay dead!"

Carley let off one shot when she said the word dead, but Lexxy already knew the drill. She'd been shot before, and she wasn't going to let that happen again. She ducked down as soon as Carley pointed the gun in her direction.

"Carley, chill!"

"Hell nah, I ain't chillin'. I tried to kill this bitch, do you hear me? And she would not die!"

"You tried to kill her, why? What the fuck, Carley!"

"Yeah. Kill her. I told you, you didn't know who you were messing with, but now you're about to find out. Bring y'all stupid asses on, and don't try nothin' stupid."

Lexxy couldn't believe this. How could her special day be getting ruined by an ex and his crazy ass girlfriend? Why would she try to kill her? What had she done to Carley? She couldn't think of anything she'd done to her, so why was she so angry? If it was simply because Lucky wouldn't leave her alone, that was something she needed to take up with him, not her.

Carley was leading them back around to the inside of the actual church where the wedding was being held and where the guests were. Cocaine was standing down there with his gun pointed, him and his "guests" who were actually security had their guns pointed in the direction of the men who were poorly dressed in street clothes.

"Lexxy, take yo' stupid ass on down there with your man. Let her through!" Carley yelled as Lexxy stumbled to get down the aisle to Cocaine. With guns pointed everywhere, she didn't know what would happen. She didn't want to get hurt, or worse, someone do something to Cocaine. She loved him with everything inside of her, and this could not be happening once again.

"Baby, what's happening?" Lexxy asked as Cocaine wiped the tears that were falling from her beautifully make up painted face.

"Just be quiet, baby and get behind me."

Lexxy did as she was told and went behind Cocaine for safety.

"Now, this is how this is gon' go, Lucky. You gon' bring yo' stupid ass home with me, and we gon' let these nice people get married, or else, the Lischey Mob gon' let loose in this bitch!"

Cocaine's eyes got wide. The Lischey Mob was a name he hadn't heard in a very long time, but this type of shit was how you started a war. He hadn't realized it until after he heard the name Lischey Mob that he recognized two of the members. They were the sons of the leader of the gang, Paul and Quentin.

"So, what's this all about? Lucky, or some other shit?"

Paul took a step forward, ready to pop one in Cocaine's ass, but Carley quickly interrupted him.

"Nah, Paul, I got this."

"I came here to get my man, but if I get to take one of y'all out, I'll be winning too. Matter of fact, where is your daddy, Lexxy? Where is Dutch's bitch ass?"

Lexxy wondered the same thing herself. Where was Dutch? She looked around the atrium and didn't see anyone. She could see as far as the church steps; the idiots didn't even close the doors. She looked into the faces of her guests and felt terrible. How could she have let something like this happen? How could these people be ruining her special day, and where the fuck were Wild Bill and Dutch when you really needed them niggas?

After Dutch knocked Wild Bill out, he heard commotion coming from the inside of the church, so he peaked his head in to see what was going on.

Where was Junie and Ella Mae? They were nowhere in sight, but that wasn't the only thing he noticed. He saw Paul, Quentin, and Carley, and he knew some shit was about to go down. Now, he regretted knocking Wild Bill out because he definitely couldn't take down the Lischey Mob by himself, nor without Wild Bill. He knew their weaknesses; this wouldn't be the first time they'd gone up against them, and this was a direct violation against their peace treaty.

Dutch snuck out and went back to the room where Wild Bill was now waking up. He jumped up from the ground, ready to go a few rounds with Dutch, but Dutch quickly stopped him.

"Nigga, we ain't got time for that. The Lischey Mob is holdin' the church up, and I ain't see Junie or that damn grandmother of Cocaine's. Lexxy told me they'd be sitting together, and I could sit with them. I went to see where they were at, and they were nowhere to be found."

Wild Bill shook his head, trying to get his mind around what was happening. How was this so? The Lischey Mob? He thought they had an agreement.

It had been a long time since Dutch and Wild Bill had to team up, but they would do anything for their daughter to make sure she was safe and happy, and if a few heads had to roll to make it so, then it would be.

"You strapped?" Dutch asked Wild Bill, who was furious. He couldn't tell if he was angrier about the wedding being ruined, or Dutch getting the one up on him.

"You know I am, hold up."

Wild Bill went into the closet. He didn't want to get his gun out like that. He didn't want to carry it around, and he wasn't going to, but now he was glad that he didn't leave it at all.

Wild Bill reached into the closet, got out his two guns, and was ready to take these niggas head on. They would never know what hit them.

***

"It's going to be ok; we just need to stay here and be quiet," Junie said as they sat behind the choir stand, being as quiet as possible. Junie was holding on to Ella Mae, who actually wasn't afraid. This wasn't the first time she'd come face to face with a possible hostage situation; she just hoped they came out ok.

"I'm not worried, baby. If it's my time to go, I lived a long life. I'm not afraid. I'm willing to die behind mine, I just hope you are too."

"I was bred for this shit, Ella Mae. Ain't no bitch in my blood."

"Good. Then why are we sitting back here instead of out there?"

That was a good point, and Junie couldn't disagree with it. Junie and Ella Mae appeared from the bottom of the choir stand, and they joined Cocaine and Lexxy. If one was going to die, they would all die. Their loyalty, their allegiance to one another was strong enough to see them through any battle, any fight, anything, as long as they stood together.

Junie joined hands with Lexxy, and Lexxy with Ella Mae.

None of them knew what was to come of the present situation, but Lexxy hoped that no one ended up dead, shot, hurt, or broken, especially her.

She now regretted not carrying a gun. She regretted appearing so dainty, so…so vulnerable. If Lexxy made it out of this situation, she was going to fuck Carley's ass up, and if Carley didn't kill Lucky, she would do it herself.

It was in that moment that she was glad that Denise hadn't come out of the room just yet. Her being drunk just might save her life, and she hoped with everything in her that she stayed where she was.

Losing any of them would be a blow to the gut, and Lexxy couldn't take any more of that.

Lexxy looked out into the faces of her enemies, memorizing each one, feature by feature, because before all of this was over, before she went forward with her life, she would have all of their heads for this damn indiscretion.

Cocaine looked out the door and waited for the gorilla faced man to leave. How could he have done this? His father was supposed to be like a superhero, surely, he would just jump right back up, but when Cocaine went to his side and saw all the blood coming from his body, he didn't know what to do. He couldn't help his father even though he wanted to. He wanted to save his life, but he couldn't.

Unfortunately, his father had trained him for a moment such as this. Juaqeen had told him in case something like this was to ever happen for him to go home and get Leon. He was the Alfred type from Batman. He was more than a butler, and even more than a friend; he was considered family.

Cocaine took one last look at his father and kissed him on the forehead. He whispered in his ear, telling him he'd see him again in the next lifetime, grabbed the car keys to his father's vehicle, and jumped in the driver's seat.

At ten-years-old, Cocaine was pretty tall, and he had seen his father drive a million times. Juaqeen had often let Cocaine ride in his lap and drive when they were just going around the block or to the store quickly, and because of this, Cocaine knew a little something about driving a car, hopefully enough to make it home.

Cocaine started the car and let the engine roar underneath his feet. He pulled his seat up, angling it just right for him to reach the *pedals and to see over the dashboard. When he was comfortable, he checked his mirror like he'd seen Juaqeen do and like he'd been told to do many times himself when his father would give him his premature driving lessons.*

His hands shook in fear as he tried putting on the seatbelt. The day's events had him shook up. Before his revenge plot was birthed, all he felt was fear and inadequate. He felt poorly for not being able to do anything, for not being able to fix his father or help him when he needed him most, but his father had told him before that Leon would know what to do—all he had to do was make it home.

It was well in the afternoon now, and Cocaine hoped he wouldn't be caught by the police in traffic. He knew how pigs could be, and that would be a terrible ending to an already fucked up day.

Cocaine drove carefully and cautiously, thinking about his father and how to get home, tears pouring from his eyes every second. He was more than tired, more than sad; this feeling that was rumbling inside him was something that he'd never experienced before. It was a feeling that he would later realize was rage.

Finally, pulling up to his house, the gates around his beautiful home opened once they saw Juaqeen's car in view, but when Cocaine pulled into the archway of the driveway, he was stopped by one of the security guards.

"Oh man, Coco, you stole your dad's car? That nigga is gon' flip the fuck out. Come on, where's he at? Let me take the car back so he don't have a fuckin' fit."

Stanley, the lead security of the house said. Juaqeen had ditched his security for the day because he wanted to be alone with Cocaine. This was the first time he'd ever broken his own rule, and it cost him his life.

Stanley continued talking, but Cocaine was completely out of it.

Stanley's words went in one ear and out the other, and it sounded more like he was going through a tunnel.

"Cocaine? You good, kid?" Stanley asked as he snapped his fingers at him.

Cocaine looked at Stanley in the eye and got out of the car. His only mission was to get inside the house. He had to get to Leon.

He pushed passed Stanley and took off running toward the house. He had never run so fast in his life, but he looked like he had dust coming off the back of his clothes. When he reached the front door, Leon was already coming outside. He'd seen Juaqeen's car pulling up in the driveway, and he wondered where he had been. He was also going to give him an earful about leaving his security detail at home, but when he saw Cocaine running up the stairs to the house and instantly flew into his arms, he knew his verbal lashing would have to wait.

"What's wrong, Coco?" Leon wrapped his arms around him. Leon had been a part of their family for a very long time. His father served Cocaine's father, and when his father passed away, he took over. Leon and Juaqeen were raised as brothers, not really as servant and master. Though Leon knew his place, Juaqeen always showed him so much respect and love, and for that, Leon would never leave, and he would always do what was necessary for the people he loved so much.

Leon stroked Cocaine's back for a moment, and then he led him into the house. Cocaine was so upset, and he didn't want to embarrass him by leaving him outside to tell him his business.

He closed the door behind them and led Cocaine to the couch where he could sit down and relax, but when he tried to get up so he could get them two glasses of lemonade, Cocaine grabbed onto his yellow sweater and snatched him back toward him.

Leon hadn't ever seen him this upset, not once in his entire life, so he pulled him closer to him and rocked him until Cocaine was ready to tell him what happened, but after a few minutes of consistent crying, he figured he wasn't going to get anywhere if he didn't ask.

"What's wrong, Coco? What happened? Where's Juaqeen?"

"The...the gorilla man...he shot pops...he...Leon..."

Cocaine was having a hard time reliving the events he'd witnessed before his very eyes, and telling them, it was too hard. Saying it out loud did more than make it real; it meant that something would have to be done about it, that there would have to be a funeral. Cocaine thought his father truly was immortal and that nothing would ever happen to him. How could this happen to Juaqeen? His father was mighty, a god in all respects, and he shouldn't have gone out the way he did.

Leon didn't understand all the details, but he got the most important parts like how Juaqeen was shot by a man with a gorilla tattoo on his face, and Leon knew exactly who that was. He told Juaqeen not to trust Dutch, not to let him in his circle, but he did it anyway, thinking that Dutch was just a nigga who wanted to end up on top, the type who was loyal, but he wasn't. He was out for himself.

After Cocaine finally calmed down, he was able to tell Leon the rest of the story, and Leon just couldn't believe this; how could his friend, someone who was like a brother to him, but also like a god, be put down like a dog? Leon rubbed Cocaine's back and told him not to worry, that he would take care of everything that needed to be done.

Leon waited until Cocaine fell asleep on the couch after all the crying he had done, and then he went to make his moves. His first order of business was going to collect Juaqeen's body. He didn't want anyone to discover it and mutilate him, so he had *some of the security follow him to the location Cocaine had given him.*

He took a deep breath before walking in. He didn't know how bad the scene would be when he discovered his body, and he knew no matter how much time he took on the outside, it wasn't going to prepare him to see what would lie in front of him.

Leon walked into the warehouse not knowing what to expect, but the further he got inside, he could see the blood droplets leading in a line somewhere, which was odd.

He followed the trail of blood closely, wanting to see where it would lead. At the end, a few steps away from it, he found Juaqeen who was crouched over, holding himself.

Leon ran trying to help his friend. The security swarmed the inside, checking to make sure it was clear, and the others guarded the door to make sure no one came inside.

"Juaqeen? What the hell?"

Leon put his head to Juaqeen's chest, and surprisingly, he still had a heartbeat. How could this be so? Cocaine said he was dead.

"Juaqeen, can you hear me?"

He was nonresponsive, and didn't even move, but if he had a heartbeat, and a pulse, he was definitely still alive.

Leon was thankful for cell phones. Had this been just a few years earlier, this could've been even worse. He wouldn't have been able to call for help. He'd been begging Juaqeen to get one. He told him it would come in handy, and the nigga just didn't listen. He believed in doing things the way they had always been done, but luckily, Leon had his.

He pulled out his Motorola flip phone and began dialing the only man who could possible help them, Doctor Chance. Doctor Chance was a military vet who had seen a lot of death, but he had also saved a lot of lives, and he was very discreet. Doctor Chance always came whenever he was needed. Even though they paid him a heavy sum whenever they needed something from him, it was more than that. Doctor Chance held Juaqeen at high esteem for the way he operated and handled business and for the way he tried to help keep money in everyone's pockets. He appreciated that. Doctor Chance hated seeing his people in poverty, and Juaqeen was always trying to find a way to help people out. Whether it was by building a rec center in the hood, hosting charity basketball games, or even just giving a bum a c-note, he was always there to help out, and killing Juaqeen would be a devastation to the hood, so when Leon called and told him he needed him, he came as quickly as he could. Juaqeen was one of his favorite clients, and he would hate to see him go out like that.

When he arrived, the security guards had their guns drawn, ready to shoot anyone who dared intrude, but Leon gave them the clearance quickly, and they let him in.

Doctor Chance was a handsome man, six feet tall, a low fade, full, pink lips, and the skin of a super model. He had large hands, and his muscles were always on swole, courtesy of the U.S. Army and his twice a day work out regiment.

He leaned down and began assessing Juaqeen's wounds, and he knew right away that the only thing he could do for him was clean the wounds to keep them from getting infected, possibly remove the bullets, and give him something for the pain, but there would be a long road ahead for him if he was to survive.

"Ok, give me the alcohol and those tweezers from my bag," he instructed Leon who felt he was already waiting too long to act.

Doctor Chance carefully maneuvered the tweezers, removing the first bullet, and then the second, all the while, Juaqeen never moved. His heartbeat was weak, but that was a ticker that just kept on ticking.

He applied his recommended antiseptic and bandaged him up the best he could.

"You're going to have to get him to the hospital, Leon, if you want him to survive. I know you may not want to, but I don't see how he will make it if you don't have him transported."

"How long do you think he has?" Leon asked out of concern, but also because he had another idea.

"That's hard to say. Juaqeen is a strong man, and before today, he was in perfect health. I don't know how he's made it this long, but somehow, he did. I don't know how long he can go on like this though. My professional opinion says to take him to the hospital, but my other opinion that knows the situation says he might be able to heal if the bandages are changed frequently, he has pain peels, and the wounds stay cleaned. I was able to remove the bullets from his body, and they didn't hit anything major, but I just…I don't know, Leon." Doctor Chance spoke truthfully. He didn't want to say anything that would provide false hope or make him think that this would be something that could easily be beaten, when that wasn't quite the case.

"Thank you for coming. I know what to do from here."

Leon shook hands with Doctor Chance and watched him leave the warehouse. Leon looked around him to see who was near. Even though he trusted the security with his life, there were some secrets that your life was worth losing over, and he didn't know who he could trust with the secret he'd been keeping for emergencies like this.

Leon pulled his phone back out and scrolled down to the number in his phone saved under Unknown. It had been a very long time since he'd called the number, so he hoped it was still in service, and he hoped the person on the other end had a solution to the problem Leon was experiencing.

The phone rang back to back in his ear, and he was sure no one was going to answer. It had been ringing entirely too long now, and if the person on the other end didn't answer, there would be no saving Juaqeen, and he would have to accept the fact that his best friend, his only friend and brother would die.

"Hello? Leon, this better be good. I'm in the middle of some——"

"Juaqeen's been shot, so I don't really give a damn what you're in the middle of, man. He needs some help, your kind of help. I don't know what else to do. Doctor Chance says he won't make it without medical attention, and you know I can't take him to the hospital."

Roman, Juaqeen's father, breathed heavily into the phone, sighing, trying to figure out what their next move should be. If Leon was calling, it obviously had to be a big deal, and now that he knew Juaqeen had been shot, there was nothing that he wouldn't do to see his son restored to his full capacity of healthiness. He began giving Leon instructions on what to do. Roman informed him that he'd be sending a chopper for him immediately to life flight him to Haiti, the birthplace of their family.

Three hours later, Leon said goodbye to his friend, hoping that Roman had it from here, but he knew this would be the end of the line. He could never call Roman again, ever. It was important for people to believe that Juaqeen was dead and that he'd gone on to the upper room to be with the kings and queens before his time.

Leon shook Juaqeen's hand, though he knew he wouldn't be able to reciprocate the shake or even feel it really, but he wouldn't send him on to his next destination without one. He respected Juaqeen and hoped he would pull through all of this shit because one day, hopefully, he'd have to come back and be with his son.

After Juaqeen was safely on the chopper and Leon had said his goodbyes, he knew he couldn't tell anyone that when he got on that chopper he was alive. Leon made up a convincing story about his body needing to be flown back to Haiti to be buried in his homeland, and no one questioned it. It was nothing left to say. Now, Leon had to explain to Cocaine that his father was going to a better place, or already there and that regardless of how sad it was, he had to keep on going with his life. He couldn't let this beat him up and ruin him forever, but none of that mattered. Leon's words went in one ear and out the other. The day Cocaine lost his father, a beast was born, and though he had been caged for most of his life, soon enough, he would be let out and free and unleash hell upon the world for what they took from him.

Several Hours Later….

"Boy, you one of de strongest people I ever know. You can make it through this, my son," Roman said over his son as he let the home health care doctor and nurses work. Doctor Chance had done a good job of stabilizing him, but there was more to do. The bandages needed to be cleaned and more antiseptic needed to be added to the wounds, but even though Juaqeen was free of bullets and more than likely of pain, he was weak, and his body needed to heal before his mind would allow him to wake up.

"It be best if we put 'em in a coma fa now. That may be the only 'ting to save his life."

Roman trusted his Haitian doctor, who was also his brother. If he said that was what needed to be done, then he would do it. He didn't know how long he would be under, but once he woke up, there was going to be a lot of explaining that needed to be done and several conversations that needed to be had.

Roman looked at his son wondering what he'd gotten himself into to have his life almost taken from him, cut short. He wished he'd never left him, but it was the only way to keep him and Ella Mae safe at the time, and he would do it all over again if that's what it took, but looking at him now, he just hoped that his son pulled through this after his body healed and his mind was soothed.

Juaqeen was a fighter, and he wouldn't let his son quit on his life because he eventually wanted to send him back home to reclaim his throne and of course, be there for his son the way he was never able to be.

Present Day....

Lexxy looked into the eyes of her guests as she held hands with Ella Mae and Junie. Her guests were frozen in fear with guns pointed at them, and of course, toward the bride and groom. Though Lexxy was standing behind Cocaine, a place she normally felt safe, she felt exposed and afraid of what could possibly happen.

She'd told Lucky to leave her alone, that she didn't want him, that she was good on him, but no, he didn't listen, and this was all his fault. Her wedding day was ruined because of him, and it wouldn't go unnoticed or unpunished. Lexxy had never been angrier. She'd been strong through everything that happened to her. She never complained, never bitched, but this, this was more than one soul alone could take. Even with the support of her family and friends, it was still a heavy weight on her shoulders or a dark cloud with rain and tornados swallowing her up, always ready to devour her.

Dutch and Wild Bill stood in the back of the church, watching, trying to come up with a plan to get the guests out safely. Wild Bill was ready to bust at their asses, but he didn't want to make this day any worse than it already had become, and he knew if they murdered anyone inside of a church, well, that would really get the attention of the wrong people.

"Alright, look, we gon' try to settle this as peacefully as possible. Lexxy don't deserve this shit," Wild Bill said, plotting with Dutch.

"Cool, but don't go out here talkin' crazy; that shit ain't gon' get us nowhere."

Dutch knew how Wild Bill's temper could be, and that could potentially result in everyone getting killed.

Dutch and Wild Bill came out from behind the long, white pillars in the church, revealing themselves, moving in front of Cocaine and Lexxy.

Denise had finally come out of the room and was standing off to the side. Lexxy told her to stay put with her hands. She pushed them toward her, telling her to go on and stay out of sight, but she didn't want to listen to that. She loved Lexxy, and if anything popped off, she would be right there with her, going down in blazes too. Slowly, she walked over to her and stood beside her.

Paul and Quentin, Carley's brothers were standing in the aisle, guns drawn, along with Carley, ready to make some shit happen, but Dutch and Wild Bill weren't going to let that go down.

"Damn, I thought y'all niggas would catch on fire walkin' inside of a church, fuckin' vampire ass niggas." Wild Bill spat, making himself be heard rather than just being seen.

Cocaine turned around and looked into Lexxy's eyes, and he saw something there he'd never seen before. Her eyes weren't sad; she held rage behind them, and Cocaine knew that was a dangerous thing.

"Aww shit, they let the rabid dog out of his cage, Wild Bill, long time no see," Quentin said. He was a hot head, much like Wild Bill, and if somebody didn't control them, it was going to go down.

"All that chit chat ain't what we came out here to do, fellas. Look, as you can see, my daughter is trying to get married. We all just wanna have a good time. Whatever business you thought you had here, you don't, so go ahead and get out of here so we can continue this family event."

Dutch stepped forward, rolling up his sleeves in case it was about to get messy.

Paul and Quentin looked into Dutch's eyes and then at each other. There were several things unspoken between all of them, and Paul knew they couldn't afford to lose the business they did with the gorilla gang, in secret of course. They were natural enemies, and they were not supposed to be involved with one another, but the streets were filled with secrets, and nobody was completely loyal.

"Put all that shit up, y'all. We ain't come here for all that. We came here to help out baby sis, and now that we have, we can be out." Paul, who clearly had the most sense, gave the order for everyone to relax, and they did. Their guns went down without hesitation. Paul was a boss in his own right, and he wasn't to be taken lightly. Quentin, on the other hand, couldn't believe it, and wasn't ready to let this go. It had been a long time since he got to see some real action, especially against the gorilla gang, and he'd been waiting for his moment to come again when he could do some damage, but that day wasn't going to be today, not against Paul's orders.

"Carley, get yo' nigga, and let's go!" Paul barked.

Lucky, who at this point was just trying not to get shot, was standing by Carley, who had one of her hands wrapped tightly around his arm, pulling him toward the exit of the church.

"Now see, I done had to come up in here and fuck up a good time all because of you. Bring yo' stupid ass home!"

Lexxy started clapping. She didn't have any beef with Carley except for the obvious: she ruined her wedding.

Cocaine didn't want to say the wrong thing or do anything to further upset anyone. He just wanted to make sure his family was safe, and that Lexxy could still have her special moment.

"We gon' see y'all asses again though; that's a promise!" Quentin said as he turned around to walk out of the church with the rest of the Lischey Mob and Carley partially dragging Lucky out as well.

As the Lischey Mob fled the church and Cocaine worked the crowd to get the guests back settled, Dutch slipped out. He couldn't say it, but he had some business to handle, and he needed to get out of there before his shit got laid bare. He would regret missing Lexxy's wedding, but he had to do what he had to do. Besides, Lexxy's real father was there, so what did they need Dutch for?

Cocaine realized he couldn't settle the guests himself, at least not with what was still on his mind. He wanted to make sure the Lischey Mob left and that they were gone for good, so he followed them outside to make sure they didn't have a change of heart and decide to come back in the church to try and fuck something up, well, more than they already had.

Cocaine was glad he had some of the gorilla gang from Texas come down because they were real shooters, and however he moved, they did the same. Some of them had stayed loyal and stayed down, and even when he left, they kept the operation in Texas running smoothly. He didn't have to worry about them handling business because he knew they were just as hungry as he was. He didn't have to check his money to make sure it was right because he knew he could count on his guys to make it happen, and when he went outside to check on the Lischey Mob, they followed suit.

Paul was busy loading everyone up in the slew of cars they'd arrived in, but of course, Quentin, who was ready for a fight just couldn't let a good thing go. He'd noticed Cocaine inside of the church, and he recognized him, but it didn't hit him until he actually made it outside.

There was something like an urban legend going around about Juaqeen having a son, and if he ever came back into power, dethroning Dutch, it was going to be hell to pay, and they knew the only way to ensure that was by his death. Paul hadn't given this much thought; he felt secure in his position, but Quentin never did. He was always searching for more, wanting more, and he would have it, no matter what that meant.

When Quentin saw Cocaine standing at the top of the church's stairs, he went over to his brother and pulled him to the side.

"Nigga, you know who that is, don't you?" Quentin asked his brother who had no clue what he was talking about.

"Who?"

"Him, dude up there. His name is Cocaine, you know, Juaqeen's son."

Paul couldn't figure out why he should care about that or how his brother even knew that.

"Ok? I should care, why, and how do you know his name?"

Paul knew a little bit of everybody, so if he didn't know someone, it usually meant they were no one, but not in this case. Cocaine was a name that rang alarms.

"Come on, man, you know, the nigga Dutch took the gorilla gang from. That's his son. The only real way to get him out of the way, is to really get his ass out the way! I'm sick of coming in second, I don't know how you ain't. This city belongs to us. We done let some niggas come from Texas and run us the fuck around the way."

Quentin spoke the truth even if Paul didn't want to hear it, but Paul didn't think this was the time to do anything about it.

Quentin tried to grab his brother's arm because he knew he was about to do something stupid, but Quentin overpowered him and pushed him away.

"Ay' yo, man, they say you the nigga's kid who Dutch took the gorilla gang from. Any truth in that, fam?"

"Fam? We ain't fam, and he ain't take shit. Them niggas was never loyal which means they could never really be the gorilla gang. This right here behind me, standin' tall, these niggas is real gorillas."

Cocaine's friends stood sprawled out across the church steps, most of them with their hands on their guns, others with their hands in their pockets.

Quentin thought it was funny, that they were practically a joke, and he had just the thing to cure Cocaine of his humor.

"Check it out, we, the Lischey Mob, own these here streets. Nashville is ours, but I can see you take ya' lil' monkey gang seriously, but we can have it out...see who's the real boss of the streets. I see you standin' up there wit' ya' chest all poked out. Who this nigga think he is, a king?" Quentin asked no one in particular. Paul stood there shaking his head. He hated his brother sometimes for the way he acted. He was ignorant and didn't have any patience. If he just played along for a little while longer, he would've known that Paul was already making moves to finish taking over in that territory, but Quentin was an idiot.

Cocaine walked down the stairs towards Quentin, completely unafraid and unbothered, but he wanted to make sure he got something understood between the two of them. Cocaine didn't want to get any blood on his suit, so he knew he had to keep his hands to himself, which would be extremely hard for him to do.

"Check this out, dude. Y'all done came up in here, tried to ruin my wedding, fuckin' shit up for me, and now, you wanna wait 'til you get outside to talk about what, a fight? Nigga, I could whoop yo' ass with a $2 belt from the Dollar Store, but I love my woman, and I won't embarrass her any further today. Fight you for what? For a metaphorical claim to the streets that was mine from the day I was born? Nigga, get the fuck out of here. Any nigga that gotta claim he a boss, ain't a boss. A boss is heard of, barely ever seen, so I suggest you take ya ass up out of here before some real damage is done, and baby boy, trust me when I say, yo' shit'll stink if I leave you out here leakin'."

Cocaine's sharp tongue pissed Quentin off, and it was enough for Paul to be able to pull him away. Paul didn't want it to have to come down to something like this. He truly wanted peace in the streets though he knew it could never happen, not as long as Quentin was acting out and Dutch's ass was in power.

"Dude, let's just fuckin' go. We came here for Carley, now that shits done… let's go the fuck home."

Paul pushed his brother down the stairs and into the car.

This wouldn't be the last they'd see of the Lischey

Mob, and it would be on even worse terms than it was now.

Quentin looked into Cocaine's eyes and recognized the sharp intense look he was giving him. They both felt a murder coming, but neither of them knew who it would be.

CHAPTER 19

After Cocaine spoke his peace with the Lischey Mob, he entered the church with a clear head. Even with all of the day's events, all he wanted to do was be with Lexxy. He was still ready to get married, and he wanted that more than he wanted his next breath. Lexxy's happiness meant more to everyone there than it did to even herself.

Cocaine came back inside the church with nothing but marriage and love on his mind. He was finally going to make Lexxy Mrs. Blackwood, or so he thought, until he came back into the beautifully decorated atrium that was empty aside from his grandmother and Junie.

They were both down in the front row, holding a conversation, but all of the other guests were gone, and even Lexxy seemed to have been gone.

The gorilla gang dispersed and went back to their seats, waiting for the ceremony to start, if there was even going to be one.

"So, where is everyone?" Cocaine asked as he walked up to Junie and Ella Mae.

"Well, the guests left throughout the back, afraid of what might have been going on in the front. Bill and

Denise are in the back with Lexxy; apparently, she's refusing to come out."

"What you mean refusing to come out? We're supposed to be getting married. She betta…you know what…I'ma be back."

"Coco!" Ella Mae yelled. If he was anything like his father, she knew his next move would not be any good.

Cocaine went to the back to find Lexxy, but when he got to her room, she was gone. He shook his head deep in thought. Was she really running away from him now? After everything they'd been through, did she not want to stay? Was she not ready for this? Not even God himself could change his mind about Lexxy, so what changed hers?

Cocaine continued searching for Lexxy, but he was unsuccessful. He couldn't find her anywhere, but he wasn't going to quit. By the end of this day, they would be in Bora Bora, on a yacht, enjoying their honeymoon as the Blackwood newlyweds.

"I can't do it. I don't even really want to anymore. It's not meant to be. Every time I think we've got shit figured out, something else goes wrong. Why would anyone want to live that way? You think I do? I'm sick of this shit, this family, and everything that goes along with it. I love Cocaine, but is this worth it? When will the happy ending begin? It's like, damn, I know I'm not a Disney princess, but I deserve my story to turn out well in the end."

Lexxy vented to Denise and Wild Bill, pouring her soul out and letting her true feelings finally surface. She was in pain mentally and emotionally, and even her feet hurt. For the last hour or so, she'd been on her feet, praying the church didn't get shot up, standing behind the man that would be her husband, but now, she wasn't so sure. She didn't know if this was the life she wanted to continue living. Would it always be this way, where she'd always be just on the brink of being happy?

Wild Bill stroked her back, comforting her the best way he knew how. Since it had come out that Wild Bill was her father, he did everything he could to be the best father she could have. Though he was there as an uncle, he wasn't able to be there as a father, and he wasn't taking any shortcuts now; he was going to be there for everything.

Denise sat on the other side of her, finally sober, holding her hand, listening to her life quarrel.

"Listen, baby girl, I know you're upset, I know you're mad and everything, but you gotta just look at it like this —you were raised in this shit. You had to know eventually you'd be faced with something like this. Hell no, you wouldn't think it would happen at your wedding, but you knew some shit was bound to pop off eventually. It just so happened to be that yo' ex nigga was accidentally responsible for it, but that don't mean you shouldn't marry Cocaine. He loves you, and that type of love, you don't wanna let slip away. You don't want to be an old woman wishing you and Cocaine got married or had kids. You don't want them type of regrets."

Wild Bill was speaking from his heart. He never

forgave himself for allowing Junie to run away and be with Dutch. He wished he would have known that Lexxy was his daughter beforehand or that they had kids together before or even after, but that was a thing of the past. Even though Dutch and Junie had been separated, he wasn't sure of the dynamic at this point, and he always felt like no matter what, it was too late for him to get back with her, and he didn't want that for Lexxy.

Lexxy realized Wild Bill was speaking from experience, but she still wasn't sure. How could she be forced to believe that there would be a lifetime of happiness with him when on every corner and every turn, there was some bullshit.

Outside of the church in the back were water fountains with little angels circling them. Lexxy was sitting right beside the cherubims who were leaning over the waterfall, meeting to almost kiss.

Cocaine found her, his beautiful almost bride, and as the water fell behind her and the angels above her looking as if they were about to kiss, he fell in love with her all over again.

He took a few steps near her, and Wild Bill turned her around to see Cocaine. Instantly, embarrassment fell over her face. She didn't want him to see her this way. She was unsure, yeah, but she didn't want him to know that. She hoped by the time he found her, if he was even looking for her that she'd be feeling one-hundred percent again, but she wasn't. She didn't want Cocaine to see her falling apart, but whether she wanted to admit it or not, she needed him. She needed his strong, warm embrace to take her in so that she could feel better.

"What are you doin' out here, beautiful?" Cocaine asked as he approached Lexxy, who had tears streaming down her face.

Wild Bill and Denise took that as their cue to go on and give them some privacy, so they went back into the atrium and waited, hoping there would be a wedding eventually.

"Ugh…I don't know, baby."

Lexxy rose from the fountain as Cocaine raised his arms to allow her to come into them, into the only safe place there was in the world.

"What's bothering you, baby? Tell me now so we can fix it. I'm not leavin' here without you becoming Mrs. Blackwood."

Lexxy blushed at hearing her name that was hers long ago whether she knew it or not.

"Is this our life? Is this what we have to look forward to? Murders, disease, fear? Is that what our legacy will be, if we do have kids?"

"Nah, baby, this is just the bullshit, the test we gotta get through before we take the leap of happiness. Murder was gon' come in your life whether I was here or not; both of yo daddies got a lot of blood on their hands, so at some point, somebody would've been comin' back for they asses. Disease? Shit, let's be real, baby. You had a bad time, that's true, and you didn't deserve it, but when we old, we gon' both be diseased, cancerous, old and wrinkly. Fear and shit? The only thing I'm afraid of is losing you, and you know that, so if you ain't got no more excuses, meet me at the altar, lil' baby, and let me make you mine on some forever type shit."

This was just the pep talk Lexxy needed. She just needed to be reassured that no matter what, the two of them would be together because at the end of the day, that was all that mattered. Lexxy couldn't think of anyone else who would've stayed by her side through all of this besides Denise and Cocaine, not even Lucky was consistent. Lucky was a consolation prize, whereas Cocaine was the lottery money. She was blessed the day Cocaine strolled into that dusty ass diner. He saved her life, and if his only fear was losing her, she would take that fear away right now.

The two of them joined hands and headed back in the church. The only people who were left was Ella Mae, Junie, Wild Bill, Denise, and some of the gorilla gang. The pastor, who had been asleep in his study had emerged, and he was waiting at the end of the aisle in between the decorated lavender and white arches.

Lisa Tucker's song cued back up and played in the background, signaling that it was time for the wedding to actually start. Wild Bill had been sitting in the front row up until this moment, but he wasn't going to miss his time to walk Lexxy down the aisle. It didn't matter to him how many people were inside the church because in his mind and his heart, he was fulfilled. This was an important part of his destiny and legacy, and he wished he could have many more of these moments.

Wild Bill went to Lexxy's side as the doorways to the atrium opened once again. Lexxy's glowing, beautiful, tear-stained face filled their hearts with happiness and light, and everyone knew that regardless of what they'd gone through, this was meant to be, and they were going to be one of the happiest couples ever known.

"You ready, baby?"

She nodded her head, and Wild Bill wrapped her arm around his. Cocaine had made his way to the front of the arches just before she walked down, just in time to receive her.

As the music played and the words sunk in, Lexxy's eyes began to water, but thank God they were happy tears.

Lexxy walked down the aisle slowly and elegantly, anxiously awaiting that moment to take Cocaine's hands in hers, but what took the cake was the way he looked at her. It was as if her soul recognized his, and they were melted into one.

As they continued walking, Wild Bill was filled with thoughts of her and Denise when they were teenagers, talking about when they got married, planning their weddings, and this was nothing like what either one of them wanted, but that didn't matter to anyone, especially not Wild Bill. He was just happy to be up close and personal at this special event.

The song ended on the last verse at the same time Lexxy met Cocaine. Wild Bill leaned over and looked her in the eyes, his heart pounding. He wished he could rewind time and be there for her in the past, but that was impossible. Wild Bill kissed her on the cheek, grabbed Cocaine's hand and joined it with Lexxy's.

"You know I'll kill you if you fuck up, right?" Wild Bill said honestly. He would literally ruin Cocaine if he fucked up what he and Lexxy had.

The pastor, who was old as the church itself, yawned, ready to get the wedding over with.

"Ladies, gentlemen, we are gathered here today to join this man, and this woman, in holy matrimony…"

The pastor went on with his designated wedding speech, but Cocaine couldn't wait any longer. He was ready to say I do.

"Look man, I don't mean to disrespect you. I appreciate your portion to what you contributin' to this wedding, but if it's all the same to you, I just wanna say I do so I can take my woman to Bora Bora and spoil her fine ass."

"Language!" Ella Mae said, reminding him that he was in a church still.

"Uh, yes." The pastor pushed his glasses back on his face, flipped through the bible and got straight to the end.

"Do you, Alexxus Sade Hassle take Cocaine Blackwood to be your lawfully wedded husband for as long as you both shall live?"

"I do."

"And Cocaine—"

"Yeah, I do, I do, speed this shit up."

Cocaine was so ready to take his woman and get the fuck up out of there, and it seemed like the minutes were just passing by too slowly.

"I now pronounce you, husband and wife. You may now kiss your bride."

Cocaine was already on his way to lean in for a kiss. He didn't need a preacher to tell him what part of the ceremony this was; he had been imagining it for the last several days, and now that it was here, he couldn't have been more satisfied.

"You ready to go, Mrs. Blackwood?"

"Never been more ready."

Junie, Wild Bill, Ella Mae, and the remaining members of the gorilla gang came and wished them well.

"Baby, I'm so proud of you!" Junie kissed Lexxy on the cheek and hugged both her and Cocaine. She remembered being a young bride and how beautiful the sanctity of marriage was, but her marriage with Dutch was beyond over, but looking at Cocaine and Lexxy, she knew her future with her husband was bright, and he would die making it so.

As they walked out of the church, Denise was already waiting outside for them.

"How did you get out of here so fast?" Lexxy asked.

"I snuck out during that fifty-year long kiss. I love you so much, Lexxy, and I just want you to be happy. I hope you have fun on the honeymoon, and don't worry about anything. I love you, sis."

"I love you too!"

Lexxy and Denise hugged one another. Their bond as friends had been tested time after time throughout the last year, but their friendship had never been more solid as it was on this day.

After they let one another go, Cocaine swooped Lexxy up in his arms and carried her down the stairs to the all-white Hummer that was parked in front of the church.

"'You remembered!" Lexxy squealed as she flailed around in his arms.

Even with all the money she and Cocaine both had, she'd never ridden in an all-white Hummer and had always said she wanted to on her wedding day. Something about it reminded her of a white horse and carriage. Large engine, large tires; it was just big and super spacious. Lexxy was simple, and so were her requests, so Cocaine would do anything for her to be happy, and if a Hummer would do it, that wasn't shit. She didn't know, but it wasn't rented—it belonged to her.

"Go around the front, baby," Cocaine said as he placed her feet flat on the ground. She went around the front of the Hummer, and around the lights were eyebrows and eyelashes for her car, with red lips painted in between.

"She looks just like me!" Lexxy said as she jumped up and down. "Ooh my goodness, you did all of this on a rented truck? They must've had this already in the back or somethin'."

"No, baby, it's all yours. Here." Cocaine dug into his pocket and threw the keys to Lexxy. She stumbled a bit, but she caught them. When she went over to the driver's side, she saw a little step stool in front of the door, perfect for her to step up on for extra stability.

"You thought of everything, didn't you?"

"I always do. That's my job."

"Oh, Coco. I love you, baby. Where are we going?"

"Just drive us to the airport; leave the rest to me. I got your passport and ID, your wallet and even your favorite dress in the trunk of the car."

Lexxy loved how Cocaine always took care of her and how he never forgot anything. He was considerate and one of the kindest people she knew, which was strange as hell considering how gangsta he was.

"Mrs. Blackwood, can you drive? I'm ready to get to where we goin' so I can get me some. A nigga been waitin' to fuck his wife all day."

Cocaine leaned back in the seat and pulled on the tie that was attached to his tux. Lexxy covered her mouth, shocked that he said this right after their wedding, while she was still feeling sweet and cuddly.

"Yes sir, to the airport we go."

Cocaine and Lexxy drove off and didn't look back. It didn't matter who was there or who wasn't; they were just happy to be on their way to have some fun and to the beginning of their forever.

When Lexxy reached the airport, she parked her baby in the garage, they pulled out a ticket for long term parking, and headed up to the entryway of the airport.

"So where are we going? Ok, well, you gave me two choices. Bora Bora or the Yucatan. I heard you say Bora Bora at the church, is that right?"

"Do you trust me, Mrs. Blackwood?"

"Mmm…you really love saying that name, don't you? Of course I trust you, but I still want to know where we're going."

"Shit, as long as you're with me, it doesn't matter. Just let it ride."

Cocaine had already purchased their plane tickets, had them printed off and everything. He just hoped nobody would say anything about where they were going before they actually got to the gate.

As they went through security, Lexxy had a huge smile on her face. She had no idea where they were going, and she didn't give a damn. Why should she? She was with her man, and that was all that mattered. After everything that tried to tear them apart, she felt invincible, and she knew no matter what, she'd always have Cocaine at her side.

They got through security with nothing going off, which was great, because normally, any time Lexxy went through the security check point, she was always stopped for one thing or another. The last time she caught a flight, she was stopped because her vagina was going off on the monitor. She knew she had some good pussy, but damn, was it that serious?

The walk to the gate was somewhat far, especially in her wedding dress, but she didn't care. She couldn't believe she was going on her honeymoon in her wedding dress, but who was going to stop her? No one! She was just happy to be going somewhere where she didn't have to think about the things that happened. All of the trouble was in the past, at least she hoped it was.

"Cocaine, how much farther?" Lexxy asked, almost out of breath. Cocaine's long legs were going way faster than Lexxy's, plus, she had a whole dress to keep up with.

"You want daddy to carry you?" Cocaine raised his eyebrow in a sensual manner. She didn't know how long this flight was going to be, but she hoped not too long because she was dying to have sex with her husband, but since he mentioned it, she wasn't going to turn down the free ride.

"Please," she begged. In one motion, Cocaine swept her off her feet once more and carried her to the gate their plane was going to be leaving from. The whole time she was in Cocaine's arms, she wondered if this was how the rest of their lives would be—nothing but good times. Though marriage wasn't easy, every day with Cocaine was like a new adventure, so she didn't see why her marriage wouldn't be that way. She loved him more than she loved herself, and if all he wanted was her, he was in luck, because that was all she really had to give to him.

When they arrived at the gate, Cocaine placed Lexxy back on the ground and he looked at her, hoping she would be happy with the destination he chose.

"Cocaine! Bora Bora? Seriously. Oh, shit, it's about to go down! I've always wanted to go!"

"I know. You told me on our second date that that was one of the only places in the world you hadn't been and wanted to go. I be listenin', baby. I was checkin' for you from jump, you just ain't peep it. I knew when I saw you that you were gon' be mine—you just hadn't accepted it yet."

Lexxy smiled and rubbed her hand around Cocaine's face. She didn't know that they'd make it this far. She hoped they would, but she didn't know for sure. For a while, she assumed Cocaine took pity on her for her kidney issue and just wanted to be with her because he didn't see a real future with her, but he had proved a million times over that it was so much more than that, and she couldn't wait to show him just how much his loyalty and honesty meant to her.

"Hello and thank you for choosing to fly Southwest Airlines. We are now boarding flight 367 to Bora Bora. If you are in group one, please step up so we can check your boarding passes."

Cocaine looked at Lexxy and said, "This is it. Let's go."

The couple walked hand and hand up to the

boarding pass station and let the woman scan their passes.

Going toward the plane was the best thing Lexxy could have ever done. She didn't give a shit what was behind her. She only cared about what was in front of her. Happily ever after wasn't that far away after all.

<hr>

"Welcome to Bora Bora, where all your dreams come true."

Cocaine and Lexxy stepped off the plane and were greeted by a gentleman with coconut glasses with giant pineapples hanging out the tops of them.

"Thank you," Lexxy said as she grabbed her drink. Though she wasn't much of a drinker, it was time things got lit! She was finally on her honeymoon with Cocaine, and she never thought she'd actually get here.

"I don't know about you, but I'm 'bout to text Ella Mae and let her know we good, and then I'm shuttin' this phone off. I'm not tryna have no disturbances while I'm here with you."

"I couldn't agree more," Lexxy agreed as she clinked her coconut cup with Cocaine's.

Lexxy took out her phone and text Denise, Junie, Wild Bill, and even Dutch. She didn't wait around for their responses—she just turned her phone off once the messages sent and she handed Cocaine her phone so they could begin to enjoy their honeymoon.

"Come on, baby, the hotel's just up that way."

Cocaine pointed toward where they would be staying. Cocaine knew the type of stuff Lexxy liked, and this whole thing was all about her relaxing and enjoying the time she'd been given to live. The hotel was a large resort with three golf courses, ten pools, four hot tubs, tennis courts, basketball courts, a spa, and so much more.

Walking into the hotel, Lexxy's mouth hung wide open. She couldn't believe the sight around her. Sure, she had been to many nice hotels, but this by far was the nicest place she'd ever been in her life.

From the lobby of the hotel, they could see the ocean, blue as the sky is, and it sparkled. Lexxy couldn't wait to get in there and take some of those sexy pictures she'd seen some of her favorite models take.

Cocaine got their room keys, and they headed for the elevator that would lead them directly up to the thirtieth floor. Cocaine wanted as much privacy as possible and the nicest room available. The thirtieth floor was high-level security, rich people, famous people, and of course, anyone who was anyone. This was the place to be.

As soon as they got off the elevator, there was a man standing out to the right, ready to direct them toward their room. He took a look at their room keys to verify their room and its direction, and he led them down the hallway that held their rooms. On the hall, there were only three other rooms. Lexxy couldn't help but wonder who the other two rooms were since she knew she was on a boss' floor, but if their security was right, she would never know who it was, sadly.

Lexxy finished her drink before they even got on the elevator, but she was ready for more. Cocaine slid the key card in the door and pushed it open with Lexxy standing right beside him. He flashed her a quick smile, his grill gleaming under the lights of the hotel, and when he opened the door, they were both surprised. This room seemed more like an apartment to Lexxy than it did a hotel room.

"Coco, this place is huge! Oh my God!" Lexxy bounced up and down and then ran around in the room. She wanted to see everything. Every door that was closed, including the refrigerator, closet doors, bathroom door, and even the balcony door was now open so that Lexxy could examine everything. When she stepped outside, to the right of the lawn chairs that were clearly set up for lounging was a staircase. Cocaine already knew this place was amazing. He saw the website and knew exactly what he was paying for.

Lexxy followed the stairs down to where there was another bedroom, but it was decked all the way out. It had a mirror on the ceiling, all white bed, pillows, and even the bed frame was white. This place was everything. The bed was a California king, round, and in the center of the room. Lexxy's mind flashed with all of the things she was getting ready to do to Cocaine when he came upstairs.

The furniture was extremely modern, squares, circles, and accented in yellow and lavender. Cocaine always came through when it came to decorations or really anything Lexxy related.

Lexxy yelled out for Cocaine to come down and check it out. She just had to show him this. Now, she regretted cutting her phone off because she wanted to be able to send them Denise and her mother, but as always, Cocaine was prepared. He brought a camera, and the first picture they'd take would be of them.

Cocaine looked around the hotel and admired his handy work. He'd made this possible for his wife, and for the rest of his life, he would do anything it took to make her happy.

He followed the stairs outside and down to the lower portion of their room. He looked inside, and Lexxy was lying across the bed, rubbing her arms and legs up and down like a snow angel.

Cocaine's began unbuttoning his suit and then his shirt buttons, and he took both of them off and let them fall to the floor. Lexxy, who was still in her wedding dress, hadn't thought about it until then, but there were people who had been staring at her, and she couldn't for the life of her understand why, until now. Her wedding dress was huge, and it was somewhat of a burden for her to carry about, but she didn't have to worry about that too much longer because Cocaine had lust in his eyes, and now that they were alone, on their honeymoon, he was about to feel his wife.

Cocaine's dick grew in his pants just looking at his beautiful wife sprawled out on the bed. His chest, now bare, made it easy for Lexxy to run her gel, full set over his rippling body.

Cocaine smiled and moved his hand down her stomach and in between her legs, using his fingers to open them. Lexxy breathed in deep in anticipation of what would happen next. Cocaine rose to his knees and got in between her legs, putting his hands underneath her dress.

"Mmm…" Lexxy moaned. The temperature rose in the room, little sweat beads falling from each of their faces.

Cocaine continued working his hands up her thighs, pulling down her panties, raising her dress up.

"How the fuck am I supposed to take this thing off you, woman?" Cocaine asked as he looked around the dress. He wasn't the type that would just be satisfied by being able to see her pussy; he needed to see the whole thing. He wanted a full show.

Lexxy pushed him away and told him to scoot over so she could roll over on her back. When she did, Cocaine easily found the zipper, pulled it down, and ran his hand over her chocolatey skin. He could still smell the perfume she wore, even after she'd had it on all day, her skin held it in well.

Lexxy wiggled up toward the top of the bed as Cocaine pulled on the dress. She was finally free of her wedding attire, except for her bra and panties, which were Cocaine's favorite color, black.

"Mmm… baby, I ain't never seen you look so edible."

Lexxy smiled. Cocaine pulled her back down the bed closer to him and then knocked her dress onto the floor.

"If I look so edible, then why aren't you eating me?" Lexxy teased Cocaine. She always knew just what to say and how to turn him on.

"Give me my food then, mama. Make me eat it."

Cocaine licked his bottom lip and waited to see what Lexxy was going to do. When it came to sex with her and

Lucky, it was easy for her to take charge and get shit done, but with Cocaine, it was different. He made her nervous. Although it was in a good way, she always felt a little shy when she was with him. He made her feel like sex was naughty, but that was why she loved doing it. It made her feel like such a bad girl.

Lexxy continued pulling her panties off, and when they reached her ankle, Cocaine helped to slip them off the rest of the way.

Lexxy opened her legs, revealing her shaven pussy with a little hair on the lips, just the way Cocaine liked it.

"Don't just stare at it, put your mouth on it," Lexxy seductively said as she put her fingers on her pussy, showing her pink insides.

Cocaine opened his mouth wide and placed it on Lexxy's pussy. It was as if she was a peach, and he was going to suck all the filling out of her.

Cocaine flicked his tongue back and forth as Lexxy held her lips open. Each time his tongue moved across her clit, she flinched with pleasure. She was hoping she didn't cum right away because then she'd be very sensitive, and she didn't want that. She wanted to fully enjoy her man.

Lexxy moved her hands, placing them on his shoulders, digging into his back, which only made him lick faster.

"Right there, baby. Lick. Right. There!"

Cocaine smiled in her pussy. He could feel her clit getting warm, which meant she was about to cum, and that was exactly what he wanted. Cocaine dug his fingers into her ass, pulling her body closer to his mouth. Lexxy had her legs wrapped around his head. Cocaine didn't give a damn if he couldn't breathe, as long as he made his woman cum, that was all he cared about. He would suffocate and die for that pussy.

Lexxy couldn't hang on much longer. She was going numb, and she didn't know what would happen if she let herself go at this point. She didn't want to wet the whole bed up, but between looking at herself in the mirror and watching Cocaine eat her, she couldn't take it anymore. Cocaine was eating her up like he'd been gone on a trip somewhere where there was no food or water, and she was his only way to live.

"Cocaine, daddy, move, move!" she screamed. She didn't know what was coming out of her body, but something was happening for sure.

Cocaine wasn't going to move though. He didn't care if she peed on him at this point. He was feeling X rated, and Lexxy was about to get the business.

Lexxy clawed and scratched at Cocaine's back, skinning him with pleasure.

"Fuck! Just fuck me, just fuck me!" Lexxy repeated. Cocaine knew she was at her breaking point, but he wanted to taste her sweet juices, so it was no way he was going to stick his dick in her without her cumming all over his face.

"Cum for me, and I will."

Lexxy's body started vibrating. She was losing control, and the cum was shooting out of her, draining her energy.

She screamed as she released pussy juice all over Cocaine's face.

Once he got what he wanted, he was ready to have his way with his wife. Lexxy sat up and unbuckled his pants and pulled them down. Cocaine stepped out of his shoes and let his pants hit the floor. His dick popped out of his underwear easily, bobbing up and down like a wet hot dog. Lexxy was being put in a trance as she watched Cocaine's dick bounce in front of her, as if it was calling to her, begging her to come get some.

Lexxy crawled toward him and laid her head down at the edge of the bed. "Stick it in my mouth, husband."

Cocaine obliged by grabbing his dick and pointing it in the direction of her mouth. He held the back of her head with one hand and pushed her hair out of her face with the other.

Lexxy reached up and grabbed his dick, using both hands because lets face it, one just wasn't enough. She pushed his dick to the back of her throat as far as it would go, taking in the taste of her man. When his dick reached the back of her tonsils, chills went down his spine. She was deepthroating him over and over again, only coming up for air for a few seconds at a time.

Lexxy liked how rough he was being by pushing her head down on his dick. Normally, she wouldn't like it, but this, she was loving. She liked feeling like Cocaine's personal whore. That was part of her job and would be for the rest of her life.

"Open your mouth wider, baby," Cocaine said as he pulled his sloppy dick out of her mouth. Lexxy opened her mouth as wide as it could go, and then he shoved his dick all the way in her mouth, repeatedly. Lexxy made a gagging noise, and she pulled away from him.

"Damn baby, hold on." Lexxy pulled away from him to catch her breath.

"Sorry, baby, you had me goin', but I don't wanna fuck ya' throat up. Quit throwin' that neck and come throw some ass."

Lexxy looked up at Cocaine, not surprised by what he said, but how he said it. Cocaine was a freak, and she loved how nasty he was.

Lexxy turned around and pointed her ass up in the air, moving it around, waiting for Cocaine to take hold of her. He loved teasing her. She was waiting for him to take her to another planet with his rocket ship, and he was playing, so she backed up closer to him, rubbing her fat ass cheeks against his dick, only making it rise higher.

"You ready, beautiful?"

"Mhmmm…Slide it in, baby."

Cocaine listened to his woman, and as he slid his thick dick inside of her, he bent over her back and whispered in her ear and told her he loved her. "I love you, Mrs. Blackwood."

"I love you..uhn…more, Mr. Blackwood." Lexxy's breath was caught as Cocaine thrusted in and out of her.

Slowly and steadily, their rhythms were in synch, fucking each other like they were trying to make a baby. Cocaine flipped Lexxy over onto her back; he wanted to see her face as she came all over his dick.

He slid back into her and rubbed her nipples as fucked her.

Lexxy's face was twisted, but Cocaine wasn't sure if it was from pleasure or not. He'd never seen her make this face.

"Baby, you ok?" Cocaine asked as he pulled his dick out of Lexxy.

"Mhmm….keep going."

Cocaine could tell something was wrong. He could see it written all over her face. He sat down on the bed beside her where she was lying down.

"Baby, what's wrong?"

Lexxy sat up on the bed and rubbed her stomach. Something just didn't feel right. She'd felt this way before, right before she collapsed in the house when her other kidney was acting up. The doctor said it may take a little while for her to get back to normal, but this? This was unexpected and couldn't have come at a worse time.

All of a sudden, something in her stomach felt like it was about to come out, and she couldn't hold it in. As if she was running toward the end zone, she jumped off the bed and took off running toward the bathroom, splashing throw up against the floor and walls on her way there.

Cocaine got up from the bed, staring at the bathroom, somewhat frozen in fear. His mind immediately shot to the fear of her being sick again, to her new kidney not adjusting properly, or some new development. They were all the way around the world, and he would want Lexxy to see Doctor Graham because he was familiar with her case and of course would know exactly what to do.

Cocaine listened to Lexxy throw her life up in the toilet, the sound it made snapped him back into reality. Lexxy hadn't closed the door, so Cocaine was easily able to walk in and help her. She had her head leaned over the toilet with tears falling from her eyes. She felt like shit.

"Maybe we should get you something to eat, baby. Maybe all the traveling is what did it."

Cocaine wanted to try and make her feel better, even though his mind was on a million other things.

He began stroking her back, trying to comfort her, which seemed to be only making it worse. Every time he touched her, she found herself clinging to the toilet more.

Cocaine didn't know what to do, but he didn't want to make something out of possibly nothing.

"I'll be right back."

Cocaine left the bathroom and went back upstairs to the kitchen. He looked in the fridge, and there was nothing inside except liquor and water, but the hotel had room service. They hadn't had anything to eat that day except the peanuts and crackers on the plane, so he figured she just needed to make up for what was already missing in her belly.

Cocaine picked up the phone, dialed up room service, and ordered Lexxy scrambled eggs and toast. Their full menu was always orderable, and he was happy for that. He also ordered her a Sprite so she could even out her stomach.

While he waited for the room service to come, he tried to stay positive, but there was no doubt that he was scared out of his mind. Surely the universe didn't hate him enough to ruin his happiness with Lexxy after they'd gotten married. They had so much life ahead of them, at least Cocaine hoped they did.

T he week was supposed to be perfect, and Lexxy and Cocaine were supposed to be having the time of their lives, but she was sick beyond belief. Cocaine had called Doctor Graham and informed him of her symptoms.

"It could be a number of things. Without her here, I of course can't diagnose her. Is she running a fever?"

"She was and has been. It keeps going away and coming back. I don't know what to do, doc. I thought it was just because she was hungry, so I fed her, but that seemed to make it worse. I don't know. She's hot, then she's cold…what do you suggest we do?"

"Just keep taking it easy. It might be best for you to come home as soon as possible honestly. Being all the way around the world, and me here, I won't be able to help if something goes wrong, so you might want to get her here while she still has the energy to move around."

Doctor Graham didn't want to say another word because he didn't actually know if there was anything wrong with her. For all he knew, the kidney just needed time to continue settling in, and the symptoms she was having were identical to symptoms most transplant patients had. The doctor didn't want to worry Cocaine, but he also didn't want to jump the gun.

Lexxy sat in the large bed, queasy as ever. She didn't know what could possibly be wrong with her, but she missed her mother dearly. Her mom always knew how to take care of a stomachache, and she was really good at comforting her, not that Cocaine was doing a bad job, she was just used to her mother being there.

"I miss Mom. She would know what to do, and she would probably make me some of that soup. You know which one?"

"The one with the letters in it? You a big ass kid, Lexxy."

Cocaine got in bed and snuggled up against Lexxy as she started talking about her mother and how she was going to call her. Cocaine thought about his mother, and he wondered what she would be like if she was still here. Though Cocaine had no idea what happened to her or who took her body from the grave, he still planned to figure it out, but him marrying Lexxy was number one on his list of things that needed to be taken care of, and now that it had been, he could do whatever necessary to figure out what happened and how something like that could have possibly happened.

Though he was listening to Lexxy, his thoughts overtook her voice, and he needed to get this off his mind.

"Lexxy," Cocaine interrupted her and asked a question, "who do you think would take my mama's body out of a grave? You think somebody did that shit on purpose, to piss me off, or you think it was random?"

Lexxy rolled over and looked at Cocaine and thought about the question he was asking her. She had thought about this time and time again herself, and if she didn't know any better, she'd say it was Dutch who did it. She knew he was busy trying to get revenge on everyone around him for everything that had been done, but she chose to keep that little piece of information to herself in hopes that when she did speak with her mother, she could possibly find out for her.

Junie hadn't been in the same house with Dutch for a long time, but once he got over himself a little bit, they did talk on the phone. They occasionally texted, and she was still fairly close with him. Lexxy knew if she asked her mom and her mom asked Dutch, and regardless of what he said, whether it was the truth or a lie, Junie would still know. After all, they'd been together for over twenty years.

"I don't know, baby. I mean, it could've been random, and then again, it could've been something that was directly being done to you. We'll find her body and rebury her, maybe put her in a mausoleum this time so we don't have to ever worry about this again."

Lexxy ran her fingers across Cocaine's back as he fell deep into thought. Since they'd been in Bora Bora, they hadn't even been able to leave their room really. They'd gone swimming, played golf, and went to the restaurants within the vicinity, but five days had passed, and Lexxy wasn't able to have much fun without getting sick. She wanted to start preparing for the worst, so she called Junie to let her know how she was feeling and to see if she'd be able to help find out if Dutch had anything to do with Cocaine's mother or not.

Their phones had been inside of a bag the entire time because they weren't going to be using them this week, or they weren't supposed to have to, but when Cocaine pulled his out, he also pulled Lexxy's out, so she was able to just lean over and grab it and get back comfortable on the bed.

Lexxy glanced at Cocaine out of the corner of her eye. She hoped he would just get out of bed and go find something to do, but he just wanted to lay up under her, so unfortunately, he was going to have to hear what she was going to say to her mother.

Lexxy turned her phone back on, and the more she tried to get to her call log, the more her phone lagged. She had text messages, Facebook notifications, voicemails, and emails going off on her phone. All she wanted to do was make a simple call, but she'd have to wait because her phone was being stupid. Luckily for Lexxy, Cocaine sensed the aggravation in her mood from her lagging phone and decided to get out of bed and go get something to drink.

"You want me to get you somethin'?"

"Yes, please, but I want it with ice whatever you get. Just go on down the hall and get some ice. Ooh, and while you're out there, you can get me some chocolate too. I know I shouldn't eat any, but I really want it, baby," Lexxy lied. She just wanted to stall him long enough so she could make her phone call and ask her question to her mother.

"Yeah, alright, I'll see what I can come up with."

Cocaine got off the bed and smiled at Lexxy. He knew she was up to something; he just didn't know what. She wasn't a good liar, so every time she even looked like she was going to keep something from him, he knew about it. He just didn't think everything was worth busting her over.

Once Cocaine went downstairs, Lexxy figured regardless of what was going on with her phone, she had a solid eight minutes to say everything she needed to and allow her mother to answer her question before Cocaine came back.

Lexxy dialed her mother's number and went straight into the conversation as soon as she picked up. "Mama, I don't have a lot of time, but I need to ask you something. Is it possible Daddy dug up Cocaine's mom's body and had it moved somewhere or further disposed of?"

Junie had no idea where any of this was coming from, and she needed more details if she was going to answer the question.

"I need you to tell me a little more information, baby. What do you mean?"

Lexxy went on to tell her mother about her trip to Texas and what Cocaine came back and told her. Dutch was the only person she would think would want a problem with him, or had a problem with him to further make worse, but again, she didn't want to say anything unless she knew the facts or if she had some way of proving it.

"I mean, with everything that's happened, I can't say he wouldn't or did, but because I don't know, I have to say I don't know, you know? I could always ask, I suppose, and I guess I should ask today since things are probably about to change."

"Change? What do you mean, change?" Lexxy wondered what the hell her mother was talking about.

"Yes, baby, change. Today, well, tonight, Wild Bill and I are going on a date, our fourth date. We've been going out since the day after the wedding."

"Going out? What are y'all, teenagers? Mama, now that is some major tea that you need to spill!"

"No tea to spill. You know that's your father, you know how you got here. Bodda-big, bodda-boom. I mean, the only reason Wild Bill and I never got back together was because I was with your father, but now, well, now that we're about to get a divorce, I'm not going to be miserable anymore. I'm going to live my life to the fullest, and that's the end of that."

Lexxy looked into the phone as if she could see her mother. She was so proud of her for saying that. She truly just wanted her to be happy, no matter what that meant, and if being with her father would make her happy, then cool. It was strange to her to call Wild Bill her father; she wasn't there yet, although he was. She loved him the same, if not more now knowing the truth, but that didn't take away the feelings she had toward Dutch. He raised her, gave her a home, clothed her, fed her, bathed her, and even loved her, and though he'd been acting strange, she could forgive him. She'd even forgiven him for killing Juaqeen, but what she wouldn't let go, if it was true, what he did to Cocaine's mother. If he did something to her body, she would lose it on him.

Lexxy had been letting a lot of people slide recently, but that would be the end. She would flip the fuck out on him and kill him herself.

"Well, I would say use protection, but uhm...I guess I might be too late for that." Lexxy asked more instead of saying it. She was hoping Wild Bill and her mother hadn't been getting down and dirty, but she was the one who mentioned her conception.

"I'm grown. Mind yours and let me mind mine. You should call Bill soon though. The first two dates were ruined with conversation of you all damn night."

"Ok, but how did this even happen though? Hold on, wait till Cocaine gets back in here with my drink. This is tea, baby!"

"Alexxus, I am not Denise. Get off my damn phone!"

"Yeah, but who else you gon' gossip with about your new-old man then? Please tell me!"

Lexxy had completely forgotten about her not feeling good. Her mother was dropping bombs on her ass. She wondered since she found out about Wild Bill being her father if Junie would give him another chance or if they really wanted to be together. She'd always noticed the chemistry between the two, but she chalked it up to their history of friendship, but now she knew differently.

"Ok, ok, but listen, I'm too old to be getting a brother or sister, so please, for the love of all things good and holy USE A CONDOM! Or get that shit taken out. I cannot, I cannot. Do you understand me?"

"Goodbye, Alexxus."

Lexxy heard three loud beeps in her ear before she got to finish the conversation, but at least her mother said she would ask Dutch about Cocaine's mother. When

Cocaine came back in the room, Lexxy had the biggest smile on her face.

"What's gotten into you, baby?" he asked as he handed her the drink he'd gotten for her.

"Oh, baby. I just learned it's never too late to find love. Wild Bill and Mama are going on a date."

Cocaine spit his drink back into his cup. He was just as surprised as she was.

"I know, I know!"

"Hell nah, call her back and tell her she better not be fuckin' up in there without no protection. She gon' be like sixty with a newborn."

"How old do you think my mama is?" Lexxy lightly punched Cocaine in the arm.

Before then, Lexxy was still feeling like shit, but now, she felt up to the day and wanted to get out and enjoy the island. She overheard Cocaine on the phone with Doctor Graham earlier that day about how she needed to get home ASAP, but she hoped she still had a few hours left to play around.

Though Lexxy had pretty much ruined their honeymoon, she was still happy to be there with Cocaine and hoped they could somehow still salvage what was left before it was time for them to go.

"Shit, I don't know, but she ain't that damn young. Poppin' ha old pussy for ya' pops. You know what, I can't say nothin', 'cuz I'ma be blowin' ya' back out 'til you ain't got no back to blow, baby!"

Cocaine attacked Lexxy with dozens of kisses. He loved her so much, and it was good to see her finally feeling like herself.

Most people would've left Lexxy with all the problems she had, but not Cocaine. He would never leave her, ever. She was his angel, and whether she knew it or not, she saved him from a lifetime of unhappiness.

SEPTEMBER 2003....

"Come on in here and have a seat, boys!" Quentin and Paul's father, Amir said.

Paul, who was twelve, helped Quentin, who was nine, into the chair at the round table. This was the first time they'd ever been allowed to come in here when their father was going to have a meeting, and they didn't want to miss it. Their father even had them dress in little suits so that they could be as professional as possible.

"You boys are dressed for success. Now remember, you're just here to listen, and listen well. One day, this will all be yours, and when the time comes, it might come at an unexpected moment. I don't want you boys to be lost in this world. Paul, it's your job to always take care of Quentin, always. Remember that. Quentin, you take care of Carley. If everybody stays on their person, it'll never be a problem. Think of it as a buddy system."

The boys nodded their heads as their father spoke. They had so much respect and love for him. They hoped there would never be a day where they had to live without their father. Quentin hoped they'd all go at the same time. Paul didn't care one way or another. He knew this life wasn't promised to anyone, and his main goal was to do what his father had always told him—to take care of Quentin.

As they sat at the table, members of their father's organization *came rushing in, taking seats at the table. Paul was very excited to learn about their father's business; he hoped to be just like him one day.*

The men spoke to Paul and Quentin as they filled the room, but there was one man who came in, blowing in like a tumbleweed, seeing as how he didn't seem to fit in. His black suit with a very large yellow shirt underneath made him stand out against the other men who wore black and white.

"Who is that?" Paul leaned over and asked Quentin who was just as surprised as he was.

"I don't know. He must be important though. Check out his fit."

Paul and Quentin sized this man up, wondering who he could be, but their father had told them to sit and watch, so that also included listening as well.

"Dutch, have a seat. It's nice of you to join us," Amir said as he pointed in the direction of Dutch's seat.

"It's nice to be here. Should we jump straight into business?"

"Absolutely. You said you had a proposition for us?"

Amir looked over at his boys to see what they were doing, hoping they were paying attention.

"I do. Now, the way I see it, the Lischey Mob and the Gorilla Gang are rivals, and I want to put an end to a beef that's lasted entirely too long. From Texas to Tennessee, it doesn't have to be like that. Here's what I suggest: every month, I'll pay you a stipend to play the back end. You'll make a lot of money, stay out of the way, and you let the Gorilla Gang takeover. In the meantime, the Gorilla Gang will provide all the drugs and weapons you'll ever need."

Amir sat and pondered on Dutch's proposition. On one hand, it sounded great. The truth was, the Lischey Mob had been losing customers due to the lack of the quality of their product, so they could use better drugs, and of course, they could always use more money, but if they let Dutch pay them off, he would own them forever, and Amir wasn't sure if he wanted to let that happen. Though he was ruthless, Amir didn't believe in pointless murder, so he wouldn't just kill Dutch if shit didn't go his way. He wasn't that type of boss, but his people were starving. They were living below the poverty line, and he didn't want to see them like that anymore. Besides, he didn't have the manpower to turn down Dutch's offer. If he said no, he knew he'd have more to deal with and more problems on his hands than he could handle.

Amir looked at his sons who were anxiously waiting for his answer, and he finally spoke.

"How much money are we talkin'?" Amir crossed his arms and kicked his legs back onto the table. His other associates watched on in awe, wondering what Dutch would offer and if Amir would accept it.

Dutch pulled out his notepad and scribbled down a number on the piece of paper and slid it across the table. Amir looked down at the paper, and with the amount of money Dutch was going to give him, his family, his friends, the people from the streets, and everyone he knew would be able to eat, and they'd never have to worry again, or so they thought.

That day, Amir said yes to their agreement, and for the last fifteen years, they'd been living in perfect peace. Amir passed away from old age, but not before passing the business down to his well-groomed sons, who had since rebuilt the Lischey Mob and restored their numbers and name in the streets, but now that Dutch had stopped paying them, they wanted revenge, and more than anything they wanted to be back on top.

Dutch didn't want to uphold the agreement once Amir was gone because technically, that was who he had the deal with in the first place, but Quentin and Paul weren't going to let that shit fly. Had they been paying more attention at the wedding, they would've realized Dutch slipped out without some type of retribution. He had one of two choices: pay or die, and Quentin and Paul were ready to serve him his revenge straight up cold.

PRESENT DAY....

"Man, I can't believe y'all let that nigga punk you like that! Shit, if that would've been me, you already know what I would've done!"

"Shut the fuck up, Will! You wouldn't have done shit. You talkin' so much big boy, but you ain't neva been about it. I don't understand why you runnin' ya' mouth right now!"

Quentin shouted at one of the workers, Will. Since Cocaine and Lexxy's wedding, he and Paul had been getting clowned time after time for not doing anything to Cocaine. If it would've been up to Quentin, he would've handled him that day, period. He would've done away with him from the very beginning, but Paul was trying too hard to keep the peace. Quentin wanted war, but Paul was being way too passive about the situation, and Quentin was tired of being played like a punk.

Quentin and Will were sitting down at a table with several of the other workers, playing cards, and the moment Will kept talking after Quentin made it clear that he was just talking out of the side of his neck, he put his own life in danger.

Quentin rubbed his square jaw, contemplating his next move. He tried not to show out on the workers because he didn't want anyone becoming disloyal over a stupid ass fight, because he knew that was how people could be sometimes, but Will was basically asking for it.

"Yeah, nigga, ok. I'm runnin' my mouth, but you let a nigga silence you—the big, bad, Quentin."

Will mocked Quentin, which only made his reason for wanting to fight him more justifiable. He jumped up and knocked over the card table. His veins were bursting from his arms. Will sat in his chair, laughing, not taking it seriously, but what he didn't realize was Quentin was just one breath away from snapping the fuck out. He was tired of being treated as if everything he did was a joke when it wasn't. Paul didn't understand that they were losing respect in the hood. Well, even if he did understand, he acted like he didn't care.

The table was knocked over, but Will still sat in his chair, laughing. He was so high, a part of him didn't even realize what was going on. Quentin was like the Incredible Hulk, his veins were pulsating, his blood was boiling, and if he could've ripped his clothes off, he probably would have.

Quentin snatched his gun from his waist and pointed it at Will, ready to pull the trigger. That, of course, got Will's attention.

"I don't want no smoke, nigga. My bad, my bad."

"Yeah, it's yo' bad when shit's about to get real. You a sucka ass nigga!"

Quentin took a step forward, pointing the gun at

Will's head, but by the time he was about to shoot, it was too late—Paul was walking in.

"Nigga, put that shit down! Every time I leave, it be some shit. It's like y'all can't function without me, and the even crazier part is while y'all niggas is sittin' up in here, ready to kill one another, I been out makin' moves."

Quentin turned to look at his brother to see what the fuck he was talking about. He was always saying some crazy shit, but this, this just didn't make sense. He hated explaining his reasoning for doing shit; his brother was supposed to support him and just understand that that was what was going on, but instead, he often scolded Quentin for the way he liked to handle things.

Quentin took a step back from Will and put his gun down. If there was anybody he truly didn't want smoke with, it was Paul. Though his brother was the cool, calm, and collected one, it was also that same calm collection that made him ruthless when necessary.

Not wanting to challenge his brother, he tucked his gun back in his waist band and waited for his brother to finish.

"What you talkin' 'bout, P?"

"Y'all been trynna go about this all the wrong way. Dutch's bitch ass don't wanna pay us, and he don't wanna answer the fifty calls and messages I've left him, then we take over. We start makin' noise so he'll have no choice but to see us. Daddy ain't raise no hoe, Q! We do what we gotta do, but we do it the smart way, you feel me, baby bro?"

Paul took a step down the stairs into the basement where several of the Lischey Mob were standing around, but now, they were cowering back in fear. Quentin was off the wall and did crazy shit all the time, but Paul wasn't like that. Paul was a silent killer. He wouldn't speak—he just did it, but never without reason.

"Come on down here, boys!" Paul yelled behind him.

Quentin and the other members of the Lischey Mob looked up toward the stairs where Paul was coming down along with several other people who had hoods over their heads. Quentin was so drunk and high, he didn't know what he was seeing.

The men lined up into a single file line, and on Paul's command, they revealed their faces.

"Reveal yourselves, men."

Like a fraternity line before a step show, one by one, the men pulled their hoods off and turned to the side. On each of their left cheeks, a gorilla was tattooed right across it.

Quentin's eyes got wide; he didn't think it was real.

"Don't tell me you went and had some niggas tat that fuckin' gorilla on their face, bro!" Quentin yelled.

"Hell nah, these is pure blood gorilla gang members, or at least they were. See, you don't make joining you an option; you make it a priority. These niggas was ready to leave, and it's plenty more like it. We start making enough noise, Dutch will have no choice but to deal with us. Thank you, fellas. Y'all go back upstairs and see Greesly; tell that nigga I said to get y'all set up!"

The men nodded their heads and walked back up the stairs. Perhaps Quentin had been all wrong; maybe his brother was really paying attention and trying to make moves for all of them. It seemed as though he was thinking toward the future and their preservation, but Quentin still wasn't over what Will did to him.

Quentin reached for his gun again, and Paul barked loud, making himself clear.

"We are not killing one another. I don't give a fuck what it's for! We can't afford to lose no soldiers right now, Q! Leave him the fuck alone, at least for now. You hear me?"

The look in Paul's eyes let Quentin know once again that he wasn't bullshitting. If he didn't stop pressing his brother, he was going to push the wrong button and push him over the edge.

CHAPTER 24

With each passing day, Wild Bill noticed the same thing: something was happening to the Gorilla Gang. It was as if they were becoming tiny dust particles and disappearing. Many of the members who had been down with them for years were suddenly not answering phone calls, no longer showing up for meetings. It was the craziest thing. With Dutch gone, disappeared, or wherever he may or may not have been, the Gorilla Gang was in the hands of Wild Bill and Cocaine, and they couldn't let those niggas get out of hand; that was like asking for hell fire to rain down on the city, but there was something going on, and they needed to know what it was.

Though in all honesty, Wild Bill hadn't given it as much effort as he probably should have since he had the best distraction any man could ever have—Junie.

Wild Bill rolled over and grabbed his phone, ready to dial Cocaine and let him know what was up. Wild Bill could feel in his spirit that something major was happening, and they had to do something before it was too late. A revolt seemed to be on the rise. The Gorilla Gang's numbers were dwindling, but the Lischey Mob was growing, and Wild Bill had a hard time accepting the fact that the niggas he'd known for forever in a day could have possibly switched up on him. In fact, he refused to believe something like that.

Phone in hand, he was about to make the phone call when a hand sauntered its way across his chest.

"Bill, what are you doing?" Junie asked as she looked up at him. It was true, Junie and Wild Bill were back together, and this time, nobody would tear them apart, nobody. Since they'd been going on their dates, they hadn't left one another's side. Junie had a hard time telling her daughter that she was sleeping with her father. All of this was old to her, but new to Lexxy, and she wasn't sure where this was going. Since Dutch was missing, she couldn't get him to sign the divorce papers she'd sent him, the same day as the wedding, so she didn't necessarily want to rush into anything with Wild Bill for just in case they couldn't find Dutch. She refused to have her own happy ending turned upside down, again.

Wild Bill ran his hand across Junie's arm and thought about his words carefully. They had both promised not to bring their problems home, but that was hard not to do when something was going on in the streets, and Wild Bill needed to have the situation fixed ASAP. If he would've been thinking, he would've slid out of bed and gone downstairs to have the conversation he needed to with Cocaine.

"Honestly, beautiful, I gotta make a call to Cocaine. You know, they got back yesterday and all, but somethin' ain't right, baby. I think the Lischey Mob done either took some of our niggas or…they took some of our niggas."

Junie laughed. "What's the difference?"

"Either they holdin' some of them niggas hostage, or it's some underground recruitin' goin' on, and you know that ain't a good thing."

Junie did know. Junie was from the hood, and she knew the code. You live and breathe one gang, or you die trying to leave it, and if some of them were leaving, hell wouldn't be the worst thing that could happen to them; it would be what they would endure while they were here that would be the bad part.

"Well, what are you going to do? I mean, with Dutch gone, technically, you're in charge."

Wild Bill shook his head. He wasn't in charge at all, but he was going to help in anyway he could.

"Nah, baby, I'm not in charge. Cocaine is in charge. Shit, Juaqeen started the gang from what I understand. Dutch stole it from him after he killed him, so this is Cocaine's thing. He's been in contact with some of them here, but I don't know if he really knows them like that. I don't really know what they got goin' on, but I guess we gon' find out. It's time he takes the streets back, unless he wants some type of war."

Junie sat up in bed thinking about her son-in-law and all he had to endure during the time she'd known him and even before that. With Dutch gone, and him now not answering her calls, she couldn't even ask him the main thing she was supposed to about possibly digging up his mother's grave and taking her body. Sometimes, no matter how hard she tried, she felt useless, like she couldn't do anything to help.

If Cocaine did take back the streets, that would make her daughter a queen pin, something she hoped her daughter would never be. With her dreams of being a doctor, Junie always hoped she'd meet a fellow doctor or someone in the medical field, or anyone really who was legit, but like mother, like daughter. She was madly in love with Cocaine, and now, he was her husband—he wasn't just some thought or even the guy who was chasing after her anymore. He was family, and her man.

"Well, I guess you better tell Cocaine and let him know, huh? I hate that they just got back yesterday, and they are already about to have to deal with drama and bullshit."

Wild Bill agreed, and he went ahead and dialed his number.

"Hello?"

"What up, newlywed. What y'all over there doin'?"

"Shit, nothin'. I just woke up, Lexxy's still in bed. You know we move differently from them." Cocaine laughed.

"You right, you right. Well, listen…" Junie slid out of the bed, catching Wild Bill's attention, making him stare at her naked body as she walked across the room. He loved having her there in his home, and he hoped she'd never leave. He spent too many years away from her, and now that he had her back, he was never going to let go.

"I've been noticing some of the Gorilla Gang ain't been around. It's been a week or so, and some of the ones I hear from every day ain't makin' no noise. Meanwhile, the Lischey Mob is steady more growin', and their name is ringin' in the streets. I just wanted to let you know because technically, this is your shit, and you need to deal with that before it comes knockin' on our doors, and I won't have my baby in trouble, neither one of them."

Junie was in the bathroom but leaned back around the wall so that Wild Bill could see her blushing. Every day they were together, he kept her smiling and made her happy, reminding her so much of their younger years together.

Cocaine looked in the mirror on their dresser and stared at himself, wondering what his life had become. Something so simple as killing Dutch turned into him getting married, having a sick wife, and now, having to deal with the Gorilla Gang. These cats were nothing like his Gorilla Gang at home. If they weren't being loyal, then he would have killed his people, but he wouldn't have had to. They would have rather killed themselves than to have Cocaine do it.

But if there was a snake in the midst, or several crawling around, he would chop it off at the head. There wasn't just one person making the decisions and calling the shots for the ones who were leaving if that was the case; they were following someone's orders.

Lexxy lie in bed looking like a sweet angel, but Cocaine knew he had to leave her. His blissful week of happiness with her was now over, and it was time to get back to business. This was what he always wanted, to take back over the streets, but he always assumed it would come with Dutch's death.

"Ok, I feel that. I don't want no blood on my

doorstep neither. Call a meeting. Text me the location and make it as soon as possible. I got other shit I'd like to do today, you feel me?"

Cocaine hung up the phone, more so mad with himself than anyone else. He was supposed to still be enjoying his bride, but wasn't able to, and the fact that she wasn't feeling better, well at least not at one hundred percent, made leaving her even worse. She was up and down, up and down, and she had an appointment today, but he was going to miss it because as badly as he wanted to know what was going on with Lexxy, he needed to know what was happening underneath his nose even more.

If he would've kissed her, he would have woken Lexxy up, and that wasn't his goal. He knew she was feeling uneasy about having to go to the doctor, so he wanted her to get as much rest as possible. Wild Bill text him with the location and the time, and by the time he got ready, it would be almost time for the meeting to start, so he didn't really have a lot of time.

Cocaine went into the bathroom and grabbed his toothbrush and took it to the downstairs bathroom. The smallest burst of sound would wake Lexxy up, and he really didn't want to hear her mouth about what he was going to do. Though Lexxy always supported him and had his back, she was getting tired of the street life, and she was ready to get away from it. Cocaine couldn't blame her, but there were a few things he'd still have to do before that could even be possible.

After brushing his teeth, he threw on his sweat pants that were right downstairs, grabbed his hoodie, his

Beretta, and slowly and quietly eased his way out of the house.

———————

An hour later, Cocaine was where he needed to be. It was one of the warehouses that Dutch set up for the Gorilla Gang's operations, but after today, they would no longer be using it. Cocaine figured it would be easier for him to blend in with the people around him and a lot safer, that way he could hear what was going on around him and observe. A guilty man always told on himself, and he knew if he was patient, someone would give it up.

Cocaine parked his car behind the warehouse and watched from around the corner of the building, trying to see when the most traffic was coming in so he could blend in with them.

Finally, when he saw enough people moving, he got in the crowd and stood in the middle of the warehouse with the other members of the Gorilla Gang, doing his best to listen to what they were saying around him.

Luckily for Cocaine, there weren't many people who had seen him. To most of them, he was just a legend, something like a ghost to them, so he could maneuver throughout the crowd without really being seen.

"I wonder what the fuck this shit is about. Hopefully somebody tell us somethin' 'bout Dutch."

"Shit, fuck that nigga. He ain't neva looked out for us, why should we care about his bitch ass?"

"Speak for yaselves. How we gon' get paid if that

nigga ain't here? Shit, it's almost payday, and I don't know about y'all, but I count on my money faithfully."

Cocaine listened to the various members talk, and from the few he heard, there didn't sound like it was any snake business; they just seemed worried about their money.

Wild Bill had finally arrived, and he pulled a wooden box over to the front of the crowd and stood on it. Cocaine had text him and told him to try to talk to them, and then, he would step in and introduce himself. He knew business talk would be better coming from someone they knew rather than somebody most of them thought was a fictional person.

"Yo, yo, yo! Y'all listen up!" Wild Bill cupped his hands over his mouth so that his voice would project across the warehouse.

The many voices across the room quieted, and they paid full attention to him. Most of them had a lot of respect for Wild Bill, so what he said was law.

"So, I've been noticin' some shit ain't been right for the last week or so, and I'ma give y'all this time to come forward and speak. You'll get full immunity. Now, you won't be thrown out the gang, 'cuz we all like family, but you gon' get yo' ass beat for foolishness. What's been goin' on with y'all? Where y'all niggas disappearing to?" Wild Bill questioned.

He looked around the room and waited for an answer, and either they didn't have any, or they weren't speaking. No one in the room even moved.

Cocaine realized they weren't going to speak without

some type of initiative on the leaders' part, or without seeing somethin' shake.

Cocaine walked through the crowd, heading toward the front of them, and Wild Bill stepped down from the box, and Cocaine stepped onto it. He removed his hood and looked around the room. He saw some people he knew, but most of them were complete strangers.

"So look, y'all standin' around not wantin' to say nothin', I can appreciate. I respect the loyalty in the room, but you gotta think about who you choosin' to be loyal to. A lot of y'all have families, kids, other jobs and shit. It would be a shame for somethin' to happen to you or that family because you didn't want to do your part and help when you could."

"Who the fuck are you?" a young man in a Miami Heat jersey asked as the crowd began to spread apart so he could be seen.

"Who am I? That's a good question. I'm that nigga. The Gorilla Gang started with my father, Juaqeen Blackwood."

When Cocaine said that, it was as if he'd just spoken a forbidden name. Several of the men's mouths dropped wide open. They didn't believe him. They never knew Jauqueen had a son.

"Bullshit!" the young man challenged.

"Shit, that nigga ain't lyin!" Spooley, one of the members who knew this to be true said.

"How you know, Spool?" another member asked.

"Y'all serious? You gotta catch up on your knowledge. Anybody who got a brain knows that that's that nigga."

Cocaine smirked, realizing he was as mighty as he always knew he was.

"Thanks, Spool, but it's all good. Now listen, either y'all gon' tell me what's up, or I'ma start killin' niggas. I don't like playin' games, and I feel like y'all wanna play 'em, and trust me when I say I'm the wrong one to be bullshittin' with. So, what y'all gon' do?"

Cocaine took out his Beretta and held it in the air, ready to aim and shoot at anyone. If this was how he had to get answers, then that was what it would have to be. He didn't want to start his rule like this, but so be it.

The members of the Gorilla Gang began looking around the room at one another, waiting to see who would speak. In all honesty, most of them didn't really know what was going on. Some of them really had been doing their job and were loyal members, but there were some, a handful of people who were out of control.

Cocaine's patience was wearing thin, and he didn't have any more time to waste. Lexxy was already on her way to the doctor. Luckily, Denise was able to go with her, but he would have rather been with her. She was his wife, and if something was wrong, he wanted to be the first to know.

"Ok, since don't nobody wanna say shit…"

"Pow!"

Cocaine didn't say a word, he just shot his gun at the first person who looked like they were hiding something. The sweat that was falling from the man's head when Cocaine looked at him gave it all away—he knew something that he wasn't saying or wasn't willing to share. Either way, his life was over.

"Now, this is how this is gon' go, you pledge your allegiance to me and only me! You help me restore the Gorilla Gang back to its former glory of honor, justice, and riches like when my father ran the gang, or you can get dealt with, period. If you wit' me, step over here, if you ain't, step over there."

Cocaine waved his Beretta back and forth, designating the two different sides for the members. He didn't think anyone would be stupid enough to go against him, but you can't cure stupid. Five or six of the members stayed on the against side, and Cocaine didn't even give them a chance to explain themselves. It was him or death, and they chose death when they went against him, period.

Cocaine let off a shot for each one. Them niggas didn't even run, which let him know they were willing to die for the cause, just the wrong one.

Now, Cocaine was restoring the balance from whence his legacy began, but he knew this was only the beginning. It wasn't going to be this easy.

CHAPTER 25

Lexxy made it in the waiting room of Doctor Graham's office. This was the first time she'd ever actually made it into his practice. Normally, she'd only see him at the hospital, so this was definitely a surprise.

When Lexxy woke up, she'd wondered where Cocaine had run off to, and the simple fact that he didn't even text her meant that he was up to no good and that he didn't want her to worry, but the truth was, Lexxy worried about Cocaine every second of every day when he wasn't with her. She had to be on guard. She learned that by not doing so, she was really only fucking herself up. It was better to know everything, even the things he had no business doing than not know at all and the bottom fall out.

The longer Lexxy sat in the waiting room, the more nervous she became about what Doctor Graham would say when she got on the table. Though she had been feeling a little better, this was something that was happening on and off, and she didn't know if her feeling well today was reliable or just a trick.

After filling out the sheet about how she felt, her symptoms, and such, she gave the clipboard back to the nurse and continued waiting. Luckily, Denise was there with her, or she would have lost her mind. To occupy herself, she tried making small talk with her.

"So, I was only gone a week, but catch me up."

Denise put the magazine she was nose deep in down and smirked at Lexxy.

"Girl, girl, where do I begin? Ok, so Carley shut all that lil' Lucky shit down. She made him write her an apology letter, and she made him post it on his Facebook page. Talk about embarrassing! Then, she made him get her name tatted on his arm. I feel kind of bad for him. He's low key a slave now to that little Mexican bitch. Oh well, he should've appreciated a good thing while he had it."

Though Denise had truly been a fan of Lucky's toward the end, even she finally realized he was doing entirely too much, and he deserved everything he was getting. Trying to ruin her best friend's wedding; he must've been out of his damn mind.

Lexxy didn't know what to say. She didn't want to say anything and bring any bad karma in herself, yet, it was almost too funny to resist.

"Now see, he wouldn't be gettin' embarrassed and shot if he would've just listened when I told him to go on, and if you wouldn't have been being so nice. Humph!"

"Oh, now you wanna complain about me being nice. When I was being mean, it was a problem. I'm being nice, and it's still a problem. Make up your damn mind, fool!" Denise laughed. Lexxy seeing Denise smile gave her so much happiness. She knew the dark cloud her sickness had brought out of them, and she hated it, so every chance she got to see Denise looking happy, she would take it.

The girls sat in the waiting room continuing to cut up when finally, the nurse appeared from behind the door.

"Alexxus Blackwood!" She called out.

"You can stay here if you want. You don't have to come back there with me."

"You a fool if you think I ain't comin back there!"

Lexxy hoped Denise would stay in the waiting room because if she got bad news, she wanted to be able to properly process that first by herself. The happier she seemed, the better off the rest of them would be.

But Denise wasn't going to stay behind.

The nurse of course took Lexxy's weight, temperature, blood pressure, asked her questions, and then left her in the bathroom to fill a urine sample. Lexxy hated peeing in those small cups. She felt like they made too much of a mess, and she had to concentrate too hard to use one. It was times like this where she missed using the catheter in the hospital.

Lexxy fulfilled her urine sample requirements and went back into the room the nurse led her and Denise to. They both sat there, wondering what the outcome would be of Lexxy's sudden illness. They both tried to think positively, but that was hard to do when you were used to getting bad news.

After a not so long wait, Doctor Graham walked into the room with a smile on his face, as he always did whenever he saw Lexxy. She was one of his favorite patients, and after hearing about how she had become a doctor but was swept up with sickness, he admired her even more and would do anything to help. After all, they were technically Doctor buddies.

"Hello, Mrs. Blackwood, how are you feeling today?"

Lexxy blushed as the doctor put emphasis on her last name.

"I'm feeling a little better today, not like I can't get out of bed. I felt like that he whole honeymoon."

"Mmm...I see."

Doctor Graham began looking over her chart, going over her responses to certain answers, and then he listened to her heart.

"Ok, everything sounds good around here. Lay down on your stomach; I wanna have a listen at your kidneys."

Lexxy thought that was funny, but this wasn't the first time she'd had them listened to, so she rolled over and obliged. After a few minutes of listening, Doctor Graham gave her the thumbs up.

"Well, what's wrong with me, Doc?"

"I think you might be pregnant, Lexxy. You haven't had a cycle in God knows how long which isn't uncommon in your case, but the excessive nausea, fatigue, and rapid weight gain suggests otherwise."

It was true—Lexxy was gaining weight, but she thought it was because of the medicine, but she didn't know for sure. She'd always eaten good, so she didn't know what to say on that front.

"Pregnant? Oh shit, a baby Cocaine? Ooh...or a baby you? Oh my gosh, Ima be a fuckin auntie!"

"Wait a minute, let's not get too carried away. We'll test her and see what happens."

Luckily, they'd already gotten a pee sample from her,

so it was just a matter of them dipping the test inside and reading it.

When Doctor Graham left the room, Denise started talking Lexxy's head off, asking a million and one questions. Lexxy didn't know what to say, and she didn't want to say one word until she knew for sure.

Ten minutes or so later, Doctor Graham came back with the test in his hands.

"Congratulations, Lexxy, you and your husband are definitely expecting. If you'd like, we can get your first sonogram done today."

The world seemed to be blowing around Lexxy at the speed of light. Doctor Graham had told her that because of her trauma to her kidneys and body, it was likely she may not be able to conceive, and now she could?

She wished she could get excited, that she could feel joy in that moment, but the truth was, all she felt was fear. With her health history being a spotty one, she was worried about what would happen to her baby in the event of something health wise taking over? Would this mean she couldn't start back working? Oh hell no! She wasn't going to be one of those type of parents.

As the doctor visit went on, Doctor Graham cleared her for going back to work but said she needed to be cautious of her stress levels and diet because she was pregnant.

Denise was ready to pop with excitement, but Lexxy, Lexxy just prayed that the life she was trying to live, the normal, settled life, wouldn't be disturbed for her sake or her baby's.

"*M*i son, I tink it's time you wake up. Kairo, wake mi son up."

Roman's brother, Kairo came to help Juaqeen once again. After two years of a medically induced coma, Doctor Chance said Juaqeen should have been fully healed and recovered, and he could come back to the land of the living. For two years, Roman watched over Juaqeen, waiting for the day to come when he could wake him up and catch him back up to speed on what had been going on in his world.

"It take 'em some time to get up now, but he will when he's ready," Kairo said as he began suctioning out the drugs that kept Juaqeen under.

Roman didn't know how long it was going to take for his son to wake up, but he wanted to be prepared for him whenever he did. Over the last few years, Leon had been sending Roman pictures of Cocaine, Ella Mae, and Cocaine's mother to eventually jog his memory and help him out. Kairo told him the more he was able to show him pictures, the easier it would be for him to readjust to society, which Roman hoped was true, but what he didn't know was, it couldn't have been farther from that.

Seven days passed by before Juaqeen woke up, and Roman was

beginning to panic. In just seven days, a war had been sparked between the Haitians and the Jamaicans in their drug trade agreement, and he needed his son. He remembered how his son was just like him, volatile, strategic, and he wasn't made to lose, but Roman was getting old now, and it was time that his son take over in full, not just over Texas, but over in general. The Blackwood generation had gone on for years, and Roman would be damned if he let it end because of some war that he didn't even want, but that was what happened when you allowed greed into your world. Roman was actually a very humble man, though he was rich. He appreciated his money flow and knew at any time, it could be taken away, which was fine, but with his son in his home, he had to do everything he could to keep him protected, and a part of that was by him waking up. He couldn't send him away or even go away himself. It was time for them both to face the demons of their past and hopefully move on from it.

Roman held Juaqeen's hand, praying he would wake up soon. He had no idea when the Jamaicans were coming, or how many there were, but he knew once they came, it was going to get very ugly. Though Roman had great soldiers, there was no other built like his own son, besides Cocaine of course, but he was just a boy and knew nothing of the war to come.

Roman squeezed Juaqeen's hand, hoping for him to squeeze it back, but nothing happened. He instead began coughing wildly. Roman jumped to his feet and called for the nurses to come in and assist him.

The two women helped sit Juaqeen up in the bed. He still had a tube down his throat to give him sustenance, and that was what was causing him to cough profusely. He reached down into his mouth as far as he could go and pulled the tube out.

"Mr. Blackwood, no!" one of the nurses yelled, but it was too

late. Juaqeen was trying to get that out of his throat so he could breathe.

Before he woke up, he was having a terrible dream, and the ending was what ultimately jolted him awake.

Juaqeen looked around the room, confused as to where he was. He thought he was going crazy. There was a man sitting in front of him who looked just like his father, but how could that be? His father had left them when he was a young boy, so why would he be back now?

"Roman?" Juaqeen asked as he looked into his father's eyes, unsure if it was him or not.

Roman's eyes had tears in them. He loved his son and always had. Him going away was out of necessity, not because he was a dead beat. Being able to look over his son the last two years was wonderful, but it was terrifying to think he might not ever wake up again, so he was happy when he finally came to because you were supposed to outlive your parents, not the other way around.

"Yes, but 'chu can call me fatha, or papa, like you did when you wa' younga."

Juaqeen felt like he must've still been in a dream, like he somehow was living inside of his mind because there was just no way his father was there.

"I'm losing my mind, aren't I, or am I dead? I gotta be dead," Juaqeen repeated over and over to himself.

"Dead only to live again, son. You wa' shot, and the only way to save you was to bring you here wit' me. I keep a watchful eye over you, boy."

Juaqeen couldn't believe what he was hearing. Fine, he got shot, but here? Where was here? What really happened.

"I need you to tell me more like where is here? What the fuck is going on? Where have you been the last thirty years?"

Roman went on to explain to him how he'd been out for two years and how he was lucky he was able to save his life. He told him how Leon, as always, came through with the save, knowing exactly who to call. He hated to betray his confidence, because Juaqeen didn't know Leon knew where Roman was, but he did, but if he was going to ask his son for his help, he figured he'd need to be as honest as possible.

Juaqeen lie in bed listening to Roman tell him about the last two years of his life and what he'd missed, but before he could finish talking, Jauqeen remembered something very important.

"Where's Coco? My son, where is he, Roman?" Juaqeen wasn't comfortable calling his father anything other than his name at this point. He practically didn't know him anymore. His father had been gone most of his life, and that was something he had come to accept. He didn't like it, but it was facts. Roman spent the hour before that question explaining how he ended up back in Haiti and how leaving him was the hardest thing he ever had to do, so now, that his son was in the same predicament, he already knew the pain, the sadness, the loneliness.

"Cocaine is fine. He back in Texas; Leon has him, raising him alone, I tink. Is betta this way. This keep him safe."

"Safe? No, this ain't safe. If anything, my son is exposed now because of what the fuck happened to me. I gotta go back home. I need to get back to my son. I'm the only thing that can keep him safe."

Juaqeen rose from the bed, trying to get out, and he immediately dropped to the floor. After two years of not using his legs, his once muscular body was weak, and he could not stand on his own.

Roman rushed to his side and helped him up and put him back in bed.

"Listen to me, son, Coco is safa with you gone. People tink you

dead, let 'tem tink so. You dead, Coco is boy, no one will come for him. For all they know, he is stupid boy, not ready for things a man must do."

Juaqeen rubbed his chin and thought about what his father was saying. He was right, but that didn't make it any easier. The cycle of father abandoning son was continuing all for the sake of safety.

Roman brought out the pictures of Cocaine Leon had taken over the last few years, pictures of Jayla from before, and of Ella Mae. He remembered everything, and the picture of what happened to him was a little clearer now as well.

Roman told Juaqeen about the war with the Jamaicans that was coming no matter what, and Juaqeen was loyal to his family. He always had been, so if his father needed his help, there was nothing he wouldn't do for him, but with his strength completely depleted, he would have to get back strong and fast so he could be in fighting shape.

"Me promise, before this life is ova, I will reunite you 'wit my grandson, and we will all be a family again."

Juaqeen nodded his head and held onto that promise. He held onto it tightly hoping that it would come sooner than later, but he knew the business, and if a war was coming, he knew that was something that could last for years, but if this was what he had to do to keep Cocaine safe, he would spend a thousand years away from him.

But his heart would never stop him from loving his son, nor the bodies he'd drop over the next thirteen years. If anything, he saw every kill as him being one step closer to being back with his son.

CHAPTER 27

*T*hree weeks later...

Lexxy was finally able to return to work, and her life was sort of starting to feel complete. She had an amazing husband who loved her more than anything in this world, she got her job back, even though she wasn't ready to open up a practice yet, which was her dream job, but it was nice that she could get back in the swing of things at the hospital, and she was carrying a beautiful bundle of joy in her belly. She hoped for a boy because she knew how much that would mean to Cocaine, who she still hadn't told about the baby yet. She was waiting until she went back to work and got in a routine to prove to him that she was ok and that she could carry a baby and work a full-time, sometimes over time job.

But today was the day she was going to tell him. She had the day off, and she had the house set up nice. She was going to tell Cocaine all about the baby and surprise him. Luckily, he was going to be out of the house for a few hours, dealing with the Gorilla Gang, so that gave her some time to get things together. Though he had noticed her weight gain, he didn't think anything about it, and he loved that she'd put on a few pounds because she was definitely showing in all the right places. Her already thick thigs were bigger, her hips had begun to spread, and she even had a little baby bump that she was sporting well.

Lexxy didn't want to go over the top with what she had planned; she wanted to keep it simple, but still surprise him at the same time. She put her pregnancy test in a large box that she had left over from something from Amazon that she'd ordered, and then, her sonogram in an envelope right in front of their bedroom. She knew Cocaine wouldn't open the box unless she was around. It had his name on it. She even had a label printed off that made it seem like he was receiving a package, but he always liked to open things in front of Lexxy so she didn't wonder what something was because in his line of work, he'd been sent some crazy shit, and he didn't like keeping her in the dark about certain things.

When Cocaine returned home, the first thing he saw was the giant box. Lexxy hadn't even heard him come in the door. After walking up and down the stairs numerous times, she was worn completely out, so she got into the bed just to rest for a second. She'd been able to pass off her sickness on their honeymoon as a simple stomach bug, and Cocaine bought it because she finally had her morning sickness under control, so the throwing up wasn't a big deal anymore, and she rarely had problems with it, thank God.

Cocaine brought the box upstairs, looking at the label. It was addressed to him with no address or any clue as to where it came from, but when he reached the front of his bedroom and saw a letter that seemed to be written in Lexxy's handwriting, he knew it was obviously from her, but he had no clue what was inside.

When he opened the door, she was in the bed, snuggling up with the pillows.

"I see you found your gift," Lexxy said as she sat up.

"I did. What is it?"

"Open it up and see."

Cocaine felt like a small child on Christmas. Lexxy was a great gift giver, so he couldn't wait to see what was inside.

He opened the box, and inside were several sheets of tissue paper in pink and blue. He didn't know what that was for, but he was about to find out. He dug through the paper and reached his hand to the bottom of the box, feeling around for what was inside. When he finally found it, he pulled it out, and there was a pregnancy test.

Cocaine flipped the test on its side and the word pregnant was flashing across it.

He looked up at Lexxy, feeling like this must have been some type of joke.

"Keep going. Open the envelope."

He tore the envelope open in one tear. Was this really happening? Was he really about to have a little Blackwood baby?

The envelope opened, and he pulled out the sonogram Lexxy had gotten three weeks prior.

On the top of the sonogram, it said Baby Blackwood in bold letters. Overwhelmed with excitement, he couldn't hold back his emotions. Tears fell from his eyes.

"You havin' my baby, baby?" he asked as he walked over to the bed and climbed in with her.

"Yep. I'm fifteen weeks."

"Seriously? Fifteen weeks? That's like...you're like four months pregnant!"

"Yes sir."

"Damn, baby, why didn't you tell me? Oh shit, that's why you were sick on the honeymoon. My baby was having morning sickness!"

Cocaine wrapped his strong arms around Lexxy, kissing her, loving on her.

"But wait, what did Doctor Graham say about working and shit? Lexxy, I swear to God you bet not endanger my child's life because you wanna work and shit."

"Baby, relax, I've been working for three weeks, and everything has been fine. Doctor Graham said as long as I remain healthy, have a good diet, and exercise, I can work."

Cocaine couldn't believe his ears. He always hoped Lexxy would give him a baby, but he didn't want to press the issue because she had been sick. Just having her was enough, but now, having her and a baby? That made his life complete.

"We find out next week if it's a boy or a girl." Lexxy smiled and ran her fingers across Cocaine's face.

He was speechless. In his mind, he kept thinking about his mother and how he wished she were here, or even his father to witness the greatness of the legacy that was being passed down. Lexxy didn't want her baby born into the world of drugs like she had been, but she was able to still make a life for herself, get married, and find happiness, and she would do whatever she had to, to make sure her child had the same.

"So, am I the last to know?"

"No, you're the second to know. Denise was with me, so naturally, she knows."

Cocaine nodded his head, figuring that wasn't too bad. As long as he wasn't last, he didn't give a damn. He was just happy that this was happening.

Cocaine got off the bed and went to grab his keys.

"Baby, where are you going? You just got home."

"Shit, we 'bout to have a baby, we goin' shoppin'. Get yo' sexy pregnant ass up, we 'bout to ball out on this baby."

"We don't even know what we're having yet, Coco," Lexxy giggled.

"Shit, whether it's a boy or a girl, it still gotta have diapers, wipes, bottles, onesies, a crib, stroller, car seat…"

"Ok, slow down, slow down. I'm coming. I already know the bed I want and the stroller."

"Oh, so you been plannin' without me?" he asked, jokingly.

"I have. If I leave it up to you, you'll have some shit hand crafted for the baby, and all that ain't even necessary. We can shop at Target like normal people."

"I hate to break it to you, but baby, we ain't normal. Now come on, you done got me all excited."

"Excited?" Lexxy's eyebrows went up. The last few weeks, she'd been hornier than usual, and she was always ready to pop her pussy whenever Cocaine asked.

"Not that kind of excited, you lil' freak. Bring yo' ass on now, I'm ready to go."

Lexxy shook her head and climbed out of bed to put the clothes on she had on earlier. She knew Cocaine would take it well, but she didn't know he'd be this excited. Her dreams of having a family of her own were finally coming true, and she couldn't wait until next week to find out if she was having a little boy or a little girl.

Naturally, if it was a boy, she'd name him after Cocaine, CJ for short. She wasn't even going to think about the possibility of having a girl. She hoped if she thought hard on a boy, her baby would morph into the gender she wanted. She had her fingers, toes, and pussy crossed because a girl would never survive in that family, not with her crazy father, and even crazier grandfather Wild Bill.

When they got in the car, Lexxy sent a photo of the sonogram to her mother and Wild Bill, and just like she expected, her mother began blowing her phone up. When she answered, her mother was screaming in the phone. This baby was about to be the most spoiled baby on the planet, and it wasn't even here yet.

The next day, Lexxy went to work excited about the day before. She told everyone at work about her bouncing baby that she couldn't wait to meet, and everyone was excited for her. Though she was worried because of her previous health conditions, she had faith that the baby would come out just fine.

She wondered what her baby would look like. She hoped her baby would be beautiful and chocolate just like she was, with long, beautiful hair, whether it was a boy or not, and long legs because she knew short children always got picked on and God forbid something like that happened to her child because she would go to war behind her's.

She told everyone at work goodbye as her shift was over and she walked out to her car. Getting inside, she felt a rumble in her belly and wondered if that was the baby re-positioning itself. It felt like butterflies were swimming inside of her. So far, her baby hadn't given her much trouble since the morning throwing up, so she felt lucky.

It was late at night, and Lexxy hated driving so late, so she figured she'd call Cocaine so he could talk to her while she was in the road, but he didn't answer, and she didn't feel like waiting around on him to call her back, so she went ahead and started the car, and went on about her way.

Working at the hospital had been wonderful for Lexxy. She'd spent a lot of time being there sick, so she knew it inside and out, and she occasionally ran into Carley, which wasn't an issue for Lexxy. She didn't really have a problem with her except for the fact that she tried to ruin Lexxy's wedding because of Lucky's idiocy.

The ride from the hospital home was a short one, and there weren't many cars out, but when she was about four miles from home, still on the interstate, she realized there was a car behind her who had been somewhat close to her driving the entire time. She sped up, hoping to get away from them. Nobody liked a car that was always right up on their ass, but the faster she went, the faster the car came up behind her. She tried switching lanes, but the car would not stop following her.

"What the fuck?" Lexxy said aloud, wondering why she was being followed, but it could've been for a number of reasons. In this moment, she wished she had her gun in the car in case something were to happen, but she hated toting it around, and for a while now, things had been quiet. She honestly didn't think she needed it.

Lexxy was almost home. Once she got off the interstate, she would only have about a three-minute ride. She just had to make it there. As she was getting off the ramp, she noticed another car pulling up beside her inching crookedly in front her. They were trying to block her in.

Lexxy tried one last time to call Cocaine because if something happened to her, at least he would know, but again, he didn't answer. Lexxy knew something terribly wrong was about to happen, and before she could try to figure out how to get herself out of this situation, her car was being rammed into the side of the wall of the ramp, making a large crashing sound.

Lexxy's head hit the steering wheel, and she was completely rendered unconscious.

Three men exited the vehicle that hit her from behind, coming up to her car. Two of the men carried her out and put her into the other car.

"Be careful, nigga, you know she's pregnant!"

"I don't give a fuck. Fuck her and her seed. It's Lischey Mob all day, and anybody standing in the way of that, even a baby, can get dealt with."

Unfortunately for Lexxy, she was being taken, and she didn't even know it because she was knocked out.

The men jumped in the car and drove away into the night with Lexxy.

Paul and Quentin had heard about Cocaine coming through and trying to take back over, and with no hush money from Dutch, everything was free reign. Paul figured if they kidnapped Lexxy, they could hold her for ransom, but not for money. That wasn't what they were after. Money came with power, but they were slowly starting to lose control, and with the help of their baby sister, Carley's devious ass, they were able to get Lexxy's schedule and carry her off to meet her doom.

After a long week of dealing with the Gorilla Gang, Cocaine was tired, and he fell asleep, waiting for Lexxy to come home. When he woke up, he looked at the clock and realized she should have already made it home, but she hadn't. He grabbed his phone to call her and saw he had a few missed calls from her. He figured she was calling to let him know she'd be working late, but he wanted to call her back for just in case.

He tried calling three times, and she didn't pick up, which wasn't unlike her, so he figured she must definitely be working late. Instead of getting angry about her not answering, he grabbed his phone and keys and went downstairs to bag up some food to bring her some of her favorite snacks. Since she'd been pregnant, she craved Gold Fish and purple Faygo like it was nobody's business, so he made sure he kept the house decked out with what she needed.

Cocaine grabbed her snacks and his keys and headed to the hospital. He couldn't wait to see her, and the glow she carried now was irresistible. He just hoped she wouldn't be working too much longer because he missed her and wanted her to come home so he could lay up under his two favorite babies.

When Cocaine got to the hospital, he went right to the floor Lexxy worked on. The nurse, Jackie, recognized him right away.

"Hey there, Mr. Blackwood, how you doin' tonight?"

"I'm good, Jackie. I just came up here to see my baby and bring her some food. You know where she might be?"

Jackie's nose crinkled. It was a strange question since she'd been gone for almost two hours now.

"She's actually been gone for a few hours now. I figured she would have made it home."

This didn't sound like Lexxy. If she left work and had been gone for some time, she should've been at home.

Cocaine pulled out his phone to call Lexxy, but she didn't answer again, but Cocaine wasn't going to panic until there was a reason to.

His first thought was to call Junie, but he didn't want to worry her, especially since he didn't know what was going on, so he called Wild Bill instead.

"What up, son-in-law?" Wild Bill answered in a happy tone of voice.

"What up? Look, is Lexxy over there? She ain't make it home and she got off a while ago."

Wild Bill was sitting on the couch with Junie when he got the call, but Lexxy wasn't there, and he didn't want to worry Junie, so he got off the couch and went into the kitchen.

"Nah, she's not here. Maybe she's with Denise?"

"Hold up, I'm 'bout to text her."

Cocaine sent Denise a quick text asking if she'd seen or heard from Lexxy, and she responded back immediately saying she hadn't. Now, Cocaine was beginning to worry.

Nah, she hasn't. I'm about to go out and try to see if I can find my baby. I got a bad feeling about it though."

Wild Bill didn't know what to say, and he didn't want to say the wrong thing, so he just agreed to help in any way that he could.

"Ok, look, you retrace the route she normally takes home, and I'ma get out here and see what I can find out. I'll hit up a couple of her usual spots and see if maybe she ducked off somewhere."

"Cool, call me if you find something out, Bill."

"Bet."

Wild Bill hung up the phone and thought about what he was going to tell Junie about where he was about to be. He needed to get out and find their daughter. Though he hated to admit it, he was also getting a bad vibe from this situation.

Cocaine had been stirring up a lot of trouble between the city's gangs, so all he could do was hope it had nothing to do with that because these niggas were ruthless and would do anything for the almighty dollar—the root of all evil.

"Yes, uhm...I'm calling for a Mr. Roman Blackwood?"

"This he, who this?" Roman asked as he spoke loudly into the phone. It was rare he received phone calls where people didn't know exactly who they were calling to speak to, so he wondered who this could be.

"Yeah, this is Jonah, down at Greenwood cemetery. You told me to give you a call if something was to ever go wrong, well, I figured I should give you a call. A man came by and paid me to keep quiet, and I did for a little while, at least until I figured he wasn't coming back, but I'm calling you now because there's been a problem with the grave you pay the monthly maintenance on."

Roman was sitting at the breakfast table eating his breakfast with Juaqeen who was deep inside of a newspaper and drinking orange juice.

"Ok, go on."

"Well, sir, someone has taken the body from the ground. I'm sorry I didn't call sooner. I'm so sorry, but I was afraid for my life."

Jonah continued to ramble on, and Roman's mind went back to the day when Jayla was buried.

Jayla's family didn't want Juaqeen to have anything to do with her from the beginning. They hated him, always had, always would, so when it came time for the funeral, they wouldn't let him be involved in any kind of way. He was never even told when the funeral was being held. It wasn't until she was already in the ground that he was able to get some information on the site itself, and that always rocked him to his core.

Roman had always kept a watch on Juaqeen, even if he didn't know it, and every time he went to visit, to put new flowers on her grave in the past, or to try and pay for the upkeep, Juaqeen was always told it was taken care of. He figured that was her family's way of keeping him at a distance, and after a while, he quit trying, but Roman had eyes everywhere, and he knew everything. Roman kept the upkeep of her grave site with fresh flowers, a nice tomb stone, and everything. Jayla's parents didn't have the money to bury her like the royalty she was, and though Roman had kept his distance, he always paid attention, and he made sure to help out when he could, even if he had to keep it anonymous, and this was a secret he'd been keeping all of these years.

It was one thing to keep a secret about paying for something and another thing entirely to keep a secret about something that had been done to Jayla.

Though Roman was pissed, he knew if he frightened Jonah, he wouldn't give him any real information, and it seemed as though this young man had seen enough and felt remorseful for the part he played in it.

"Well, let me ask ya' somethin', do ya' know who took da gal? Was there a name he left?"

"No, no sir, but he did have a very strange mark across his face, like he had something there before. Maybe he had a tattoo or something else there and the scar was some sort of cover up. Again, I'm so sorry, Mr. Blackwood."

"Mhmm…me understand."

Roman hung up the phone and went back to eating his breakfast. There was no reason good food should go to waste, but it wasn't going to be that easy to get Juaqeen off his back. He knew something wasn't right, and he wanted to know what it was.

"Everything ok?"

"Should be."

Roman was being short with him, and Juaqeen knew it.

"So, what happened? Don't tell me, another war?"

Though Juaqeen loved killing; it was one of his favorite things to do, and he was good at it, it had been quiet for several months now, and he was hoping he was finally going to get a break from all the drama that came with being a boss.

Roman wiped his mouth with a napkin and then placed it in his lap.

"I tell you, I tell you everything now."

Roman picked up his phone and sent a quick text to his pilot because they were going to have to take a trip. It was like no matter how hard they tried, something terrible was always happening. Death and chaos followed in the wake of the Blackwoods, no matter how much good they did.

Roman went on to explain to Juaqeen the truth about Jayla's grave, and he told his son the same thing Jonah had told him about the man who actually did it.

"A scar? I don't know who that could be. The woman has been dead over twenty years. Why would someone want to get her this late in the game? Couldn't be coming after me, they don't even know I'm still alive. I don't know, pops. This shit sounds too far fetched. Maybe it isn't Jayla. Perhaps dude is mistaken."

"Perhaps, or, maybe it's true. Only one way to find out. We go to Texas, check it out, and know for ourselves."

Juaqeen was all for that. He'd grown tired of being in Haiti years ago, and he couldn't wait to go back to his home. Though he wouldn't be able to be seen or speak to anyone, he still wanted to be somewhere that was home because Haiti definitely wasn't.

Roman and Jauqeen finished their breakfast and boarded the chopper immediately after. The road ahead, though unforeseen, was what would eventually bring the Blackwood family back together.

Several hours later…

Jauqeen and Roman stepped off the chopper on top of one of the many hotels Roman owned. Over the years, he'd expanded with his drug money and owned several hotels, restaurants, and even a boating service. He made a lot of money, and he knew how to spend it.

The cemetery wasn't far from the hotel, so they had one of the cars that the hotel usually used to pick up celebrities take them out to the cemetery. When they got there, Jauqueen had an eerie feeling in his heart. He didn't want to believe that someone could do this to his Jayla, but he also wasn't stupid. He knew people were ruthless, but why would someone do this to her? Why didn't his father tell him before now that he was taking care of the maintenance? There were still so many things he had left to learn, and he just hoped he found them out before it was too late. An enemy's greatest strength was knowledge, and that was exactly what Juaqeen was lacking at the moment.

Jauqeen and Roman walked over to where Jayla's grave once encased her body, and inside the hole was a gaping darkness full of nothing. She truly wasn't there.

"Why would someone just take her body? This makes no sense, pops."

Roman was just as flabbergasted and dumbfounded as he was. He had no clue why someone would do this, and even more so, he didn't know who it could have been.

The two of them walked into the office where Jonah was sitting watching television with his feet kicked up. He seemed like he was enjoying himself. He was nothing like the wreck he portrayed himself to be over the phone.

Jonah looked up and saw the two men in front of him who looked like kings, and his heart dropped straight to his butt. He hoped this wasn't another situation like he'd had with Jayla. His heart couldn't take it.

"Yeah, this is my father, Roman Blackwood, and I'm…well, who I am ain't important. You wouldn't happen to have security footage, would you? Cameras? Maybe you could show us the nigga you let walk up in here and steal a dead woman from her grave."

Jonah began shaking from hearing the name, but he would help as much as he could. True enough, Jonah was a coward ass dude, and he just didn't want to die, so whatever it took was what he would do.

Funnily enough, he did have cameras, and he was able to rewind the tape back and show Juaqeen and Roman the man that took Jayla.

"You recognize this man?" Roman asked.

Juaqeen began laughing maniacally. His laughter shook Jonah's soul, but his father was used to it. He'd inherited that crazy ass laugh from him after all.

"Hell yeah, that's Dutch, pops. The nigga who started all of this."

Juaqeen moved his hands in a circle to symbolize a circle.

"And, Jonah, do you know where this man is?" Juaqeen queried.

"Uhh…give me a second to think about it."

Jonah replayed the conversation in his head several times, trying to remember if Dutch had given him any kind of idea as to where he was. After a few minutes, Jonah was able to remember him saying something about Tennessee.

"I could be wrong, but I believe he said something about Tennessee."

Jonah was proud of himself. He moved his blonde, curly hair from his face to wipe the sweat that was now dripping down his forehead.

"I guess we be goin' to Tennessee then."

Roman wanted all the smoke. He wanted retribution for what Dutch had done to his son, ultimately making him have to leave his grandson, and now, for Jayla. The Blackwood family's reign was never stopped, never stinted, just partially delayed, and it was about time they make their moves to get their lives back.

After bidding Jonah farewell, they didn't care what happened after that. Juaqeen wanted to know why after all these years he'd go after Jayla, and how he even knew. He knew for a fact Dutch didn't know he was alive, but where did this sudden vengeful spirit come from?

Juaqeen drifted off to sleep while they were on the chopper on the way to Tennessee where Juaqeen would hopefully be bringing Dutch to meet his final fate, hopefully.

As he slept, he dreamt of the one thing he wished he had, his son. In his dream, Cocaine was an older man, tall, dark, handsome, much like himself. He was happy, his teeth were shining, and he was dressed well.

Jauqueen was attending a ceremony of some sort. He could tell by the church that he was standing in. He looked around, and there was a baby being held up in the air in all white garments.

"Oh, look at papa's baby. Yes you are."

Juaqeen was speaking in baby talk to the baby.

"Whose baby is this?" he asked himself, wondering what was going on.

"Pop, get ya' lips off my baby. I don't know where yo' mouth been at!" Cocaine yelled as he hugged his father and kissed his baby.

"Boy, you better respect ya' elders, now hush, the ceremony is startin'."

Though Juaqeen was obviously in the dream, it was as if he had front row seats to a show that hadn't even happened. This was a dream, a sweet dream, that he hoped one day, he would be able to live.

His grandson was being christened, and he was there to see it.

In real life, this would have been amazing. Juaqeen often dreamt of Cocaine and where he was and what he was doing. His father promised to reunite him and his son when the time was right, and now that they were back in the states, Juaqeen couldn't think of a better time than now to try and find his son.

He was tired of only dreaming of what could be or could've been. It was time that he step back into the life of his son and be a father, whether he wanted him there or not.

Juaqeen never stopped loving or missing Cocaine, and neither did Cocaine. They constantly thought about one another, whether they new it or not.

Juaqeen was thrusted from his dream when he felt the

chopper landing. He looked out the window and saw the skyline of Nashville. It was beautifully lit, and the building they were on was shaped like Batman.

Roman rose from his seat, tapping his son on the shoulder, and when they stepped out, Roman felt like he needed to say a few words.

"Today has been a trying day, son. You know once you come back, there's no hiding again. This is it, so be sure this is wat you wanna do. Got it?"

Roman's thick, Haitian accent only made the moment more surreal to Juaqeen. Revenge was on the tip of his tongue, and he could taste it. He would get it for himself, his son, Jayla, and for every person who had to suffer at the hands of Dutch.

"I know, pop, but first, I think I need a drink. Today was fucked up, and I need to take the edge off."

"I agree. I know the perfect place."

Roman and Juaqeen made arrangements to go downtown to a place called Baileys. Though it was a hole in the wall, they served good drinks, and the women were always looking good. Both Juaqeen and his father could use a little bit of that tonight.

CHAPTER 31

Wild Bill waited until Junie was falling asleep on the couch to leave the house. He didn't have the heart to tell her what was going on. He hoped he'd be able to get out and find her in no time, but that hadn't been the case. He'd been everywhere looking for her, and still, she didn't turn up anywhere.

On his way back toward the house, he passed a bar and realized he could use a drink. He needed something to take the edge off, and the three blunts he'd smoked while riding around looking for Lexxy had done him no justice. They didn't help at all.

Wild Bill pulled up to Bailey's, parked his car, and went inside ready to get tore the fuck up. He needed it, and he could only hope once he got drunk, his mind would completely shut off, and his emotions would detach themselves, and he could do his job, but this was his daughter he was talking about. Was she really missing? He prayed no one had taken her because for their sakes, it just wasn't going to end well.

Wild Bill stumbled into the bar, half from being tired, and the other half from being high, and he made his way up to the front where he could start drinking his sorrows away.

He found himself a bar stool at the end of the bar and had a seat. The bartender, who was a large, bearded man approached him, asking him what he'd like to drink, but Wild Bill couldn't hear him over the gentleman who were laughing loudly a few seats down from him.

"I haven't been to Tennessee in foreva. Drink up, son!" the man shouted.

Wild Bill was becoming irritated with the men who were laughing so loudly, but he figured they must have been celebrating, so he'd keep his feelings in check for now and not disturb them.

"What you wanna drink?" the bartender said a little louder so Wild Bill could hear him, since he didn't answer him the first time he asked.

"Uh, yeah, let me get two double shots of Patron, and you can keep 'em comin'."

The bartender's eyes got wide, and he shook his head. He knew whatever was going on with Wild Bill must've been serious if he was ordering double shots.

The bartender stepped away and went to make his drinks.

As Wild Bill continued sitting at the bar, he kept looking at the loud speaking gentlemen who were just a few feet away from them, commanding all the attention in the bar. They were surrounded by women, and arrogance radiated from them.

The gentleman who was sitting closest to him seemed very familiar, and he wondered where he'd seen him before. At first, he didn't care so much, but once he'd gotten that fourth shot of Patron in him, his mind began to wonder .The room was somewhat hazy, but he knew he'd seen the man before, he just wondered from where.

Wild Bill got off the stool and walked over closer to the man so he could get a better look, and if he didn't know any better, he'd thought he'd seen a ghost.

"Can I help you, man?" Juaqeen asked as he turned around, looking at Wild Bill strangely.

"Maybe. You look so familiar, like someone I know."

Juaqeen took a sip of his beer and shook his head. "I doubt it. This is my first time ever being here, so nah, you must got me mistaken for somebody else."

"Maybe so," Wild Bill said as he continued looking at the man. He studied his features over and over again. Chocolate, big build, large teeth, slanted eyes. He knew this man from somewhere, but where? He began going through his phone looking in his gallery. Maybe he saw him somewhere from Facebook. Wild Bill had a bad habit of screenshotting shit that was interesting to him, so he thought maybe that was it. When he flashed back through his pictures, he saw a picture of Cocaine's cover photo, so he went to pull it up, and that was when he realized, this man was his father, but how?

Sure, this man seemed a bit older, but he looked the exact same. There was no way though, was it? But then again, this wouldn't be the first time Dutch didn't finish a job. He was so conceited he thought his shots were one hundred percent, when they were really like forty.

"Yeah, man, I think I do know you. I know your son, Cocaine Blackwood."

Juaqeen turned around, looking at Wild Bill intensely. How did this man know his son?

"What did you just say?" Juaqeen asked as he moved the women who were surrounding him out of the way.

"I know your son, Cocaine."

Juaqeen reached for his gun, putting his hand on his waist. Roman and Wild Bill both realized what he was about to do, and Wild Bill continued speaking.

"Nah, it ain't no smoke, dude. Your son is married to my daughter, see?"

Wild Bill went to the next few photos and showed him pictures from the wedding.

Juaqeen didn't know if she could cry, get angry, or be glad. What was his son doing in Tennessee?

Roman noticed what was going on, and he shooed the women away from them, they were about to have a private conversation, and nobody else needed to hear it.

"So I guess that makes us family. Wow, Juaqeen Blackwood in the flesh."

Wild Bill handed Juaqeen his phone so he could look at the pictures. Roman knew all along what Cocaine had been up to, and when the opportunity presented itself, he was going to tell Juaqeen, but there was no use in it now; he was already finding out.

Juaqeen flipped through the pictures one by one, realizing Cocaine looked exactly like him. He was everything he'd dreamed of.

Choking back tears, Juaqeen asked, "And where is my son now? Is he local?"

"He damn sure is. I'm actually supposed to be meeting him soon. He should be here in a little while. We've been looking for my daughter."

"Oh, you can't keep a leash on her, aye? Women, I tell ya'."

"Yo, unless you wanna go back to whatever grave you crawled up out of, I suggest you watch ya' mouth. My daughter ain't no hoe!"

Wild Bill's temper was about to rear its ugly head, so Roman tried to defuse the situation.

"Woah, woah, woah. Juaqeen, where are your manners?"

Roman introduced himself and shook hands with Wild Bill, trying to take the attention off of Juaqeen. Wild Bill calmed down and realized this situation was so much deeper than what was happening in front of them right now.

"Look, I don't wanna fight, we like family, but I guess my question is, nigga, where you been at?" Wild Bill asked as he took another shot of Patron.

"I think I'll wait until my son gets here, and then I'll only have to tell the story once, but while we wait, excuse me for a second. I need to use the restroom."

Wild Bill nodded and let Juaqeen walk away. Cocaine said he was en route to Bailey's, and he would be there shortly, but he had no idea what was in store for him. It was great that Cocaine's dad was alive, but his baby was missing, and that was first priority.

C ocaine arrived at Bailey's empty handed. He had no clue where Lexxy could be, and he hoped Wild Bill had stumbled upon a lead somehow. When he got in the bar, he saw Wild Bill right away, who was now sitting at a table with an older gentleman. Cocaine hoped this man had some information, or else, he was gon' have to go because this was a family matter.

"Cocaine, have a seat," Wild Bill said immediately.

Cocaine pulled out a chair and did as he was told.

"So, what's up? You find out anything?"

"Look, I've searched the city, and I have no clue where she's at, who she's with, or what. It's like she disappeared."

"Shit, who you tellin'? I did find something, maybe. I went the way she normally takes home, and if I didn't know any better, I could've sworn I saw pieces of a car lying around the wall of the ramp. That shit was the same exact color as Lexxy's car, and you know I had that shit hand mixed. I'm praying that wasn't it though. It could be my mind playing tricks on me."

Cocaine looked at the man who was sitting to the left of Wild Bill, wondering who he was.

"And who is this? He got some type of info? Somethin' to do with my baby?"

"Not exactly….he's…."

"Bill, I ain't got no time for fuckin' games! I came down here because I thought you had something. I need to be out lookin' for my woman!"

Cocaine jumped up from the table and began walking away, but before he got to the door, he heard a familiar voice calling his name, and he thought for sure he was going crazy.

"Coco, is that how we treat family? How do you reign?"

Cocaine was stopped dead in his tracks. Either someone was playing a joke on him, or something wasn't right. He turned around and stared right into the face of a man who looked just like his father.

"I'll ask you again, how do you reign?"

This was something Cocaine hadn't said to himself in so long, he had forgotten. "Strong, long, and hard. Prosperously…abundantly…adamantly. Break bread with those who can't break bread for themselves—"

"But never break your back to serve the loaf to the one whose back was never broken. Come here, son."

An extreme wave of emotions rolled over Cocaine. This couldn't be happening, but he knew this man wasn't an impostor. He'd never said that to anyone else, and that was specifically something special between his father and himself.

Just like when Cocaine was a child, he flew into his father's arms, and he wrapped his arms around his back.

Juaqeen cradled him like a baby, rocking him side to side as they both cried.

"How the fuck is this even possible?"

Wild Bill moved to the next seat so that Cocaine could sit next to his father. "So, who is this?" Cocaine asked as he wiped his tears away and looked toward Roman.

"This is your grandfather, Roman."

"Grandson." Roman tilted his head toward Cocaine.

Cocaine's mind was completely blown. Roman and Juaqeen completely broke down the story for Cocaine as quickly as they could, and it still didn't make sense, but Lexxy was still heavy on his mind, and he couldn't deviate from trying to find his baby.

"Listen, I'm glad you're here, legit shit, but I gotta find my wife. I gotta find her. She's pregnant, and I gotta find her."

Now, Juaqeen felt like a psychic. His dream was trying to tell him something.

"Well son, where do you think she is?"

"Shit, if I knew, don't you think I'd be finding her? I don't know where she is. I'm losing my mind."

"Who you got beef with? Somebody have a reason to take her?" Juaqeen asked. This was a valid question considering all the shit they'd gone through.

"We got beef with everybody, but recently, the Lischey Mob."

Juaqeen shook his head and already knew what was going on. The Lischey Mob was mainly known in Tennessee, but when Amir was alive, he was all over the place asking for handouts. Juaqeen had encountered him a few times in their business dealings and would never agree to do business with him, but he knew him, so he figured they could at least strike up a conversation and see what they could do.

"It's been over twenty years since I've spoken with Amir, but he can't be hard to find," Juaqeen confessed.

"They ain't hard to find. We can find them. We know the jack asses who run the Lischey Mob, Paul and Quentin," Cocaine announced.

"Well, pop, what do you say? We got save the Blackwood line one more time?" Juaqeen asked Roman.

"Anyting for my family, always."

Roman was always good in a crunch, and he would do anything for his family.

The four of them hatched a plan to save Lexxy, and they all went with the same intention, to kill on sight, save Lexxy, and reinstate the Gorilla Gang to its true glory.

A day had passed, and Wild Bill was honest and told Junie the truth about Lexxy being gone and her possibly being kidnapped. She made Wild Bill promise to bring her home, and he promised on his life that he would, and he meant it. Lexxy had four people willing to give their life for her, whether she knew it or not.

Paul and Quentin had agreed to meet with Cocaine, but they didn't know they'd be getting three Blackwood's and Wild Bill's crazy ass, but the plan was Cocaine would distract Paul and Quentin, and Wild Bill, Roman, and Juaqeen would save Lexxy.

When they got to the agreed upon meet up spot, Cocaine already knew it was a set up, but he wasn't afraid. He had three crazy killers on his team, and that was all he needed. If anybody was going to get it done, it was them.

Paul and Quentin came out of the abandoned house with their guns drawn outright.

Cocaine had his hands up in surrender. "I just wanna talk!" he yelled. Meanwhile, Wild Bill, Roman, and Juaqeen were in the back checking the house for an entrance in the back.

"You just wanna talk, huh? The only thing we wanna

hear you say is that you ready to give up the Gorilla Gang." Quentin of course was the ringleader of the operation.

"The Gorilla Gang? That all? Y'all took my woman because of a gang? Y'all can have that shit! Where's Lexxy at?"

Quentin and Paul both laughed.

"Who said we got her? For all you know, she might've just creeped out on yo' ass to get with some real niggas."

Although Cocaine knew that wasn't true, he still didn't want to hear that. "Nah nigga, she don't want y'all dusty asses. Y'all can't even afford to keep her, trust me."

"Who this nigga think he talkin' to? You know what, I owe you a whole ass whoopin'. I don't need my gun to fuck yo' ass up either!" Quentin growled. He'd been wanting to fight Cocaine since the wedding. Paul had stood between them before this moment, but now, it was all free reign. They had the upper hand, or so they thought.

They'd told Cocaine to come by himself, and they thought he did, but he didn't. He'd be an idiot to show up alone, but this was what Cocaine wanted. He wanted to distract Paul and Quentin so that Lexxy could be saved.

"Bring yo' ass on then, punk ass nigga!" Cocaine yelled, and that was all Quentin needed to run towards him like an anime character and charge his ass.

In front of the house, they wrestled on the ground in the dirty gravel. Throwing blows, swinging on each other.

No matter what happened from this point, it didn't

matter. Lexxy would be rescued, and his baby would be born. The Blackwood legacy would never die, and it was clearly hard to get rid of one of them, or any of them for that matter.

***

Wild Bill, Juaqeen, and Roman finally found a way into the house. Wild Bill pried the rickety door on the side of the house off with his bare hands. Splintered and rusty, Wild Bill wondered if he would need a tetanus shot after this.

"Ok, we don't know what to expect from this shit, so everybody keep your guard up." Juaqeen whispered to the men and thought about Cocaine and hoped he was ok. He would hate to come back in the picture just to lose him again, but these clowns were idiots.

When they stepped into the room, Roman had his gun cocked, going in first. He didn't mind being the shield. Wild Bill and Juaqeen followed in behind him, moving around the room. It was so dark, but there was no way they were going to cut a light on to get caught in case there was someone else in there, by some strange chance they thought ahead.

From the corner of the room, they heard a whimpering sound, something like a hurt dog.

Wild Bill ran in the direction of the sound, and covered up under a dirty tarp was an injured Lexxy. She had blood leaking from her head, her hands were rusted and cracked with blood, and she was bleeding between her legs. She looked like she had been beaten pretty badly, and Wild Bill couldn't stand to see his baby like that. The light from the moon shone in through the cracks of the building, and he could see her, completely.

"Daddy?" Lexxy said through choked up words.

"It's me, baby. Come on, I'ma get you out of here."

Wild Bill leaned down and picked Lexxy up. Her body smelled like shit and piss, as if they didn't let her go to the bathroom. She looked almost like an animal. Juaqeen saw how hurt she was, and he couldn't stand the sight, so he turned around to give her some sort of decency, but before he turned completely around, Lexxy mumbled. "Coco? Baby?"

But it wasn't him; it was Juaqeen. He turned around and walked over to her, brushing her hair out of her face.

"No, sweet girl. I'm your father-in-law. Come on, let's get you out of here."

Lexxy nodded her head, but before they left out of the house, Lexxy remembered something.

"Wait, there's someone else in here with me. Look over there."

Lexxy almost didn't get the rest of the words out. "I'll get her to the car. It's your call if you want to help whoever is back there," Wild Bill said to Juaqeen.

Juaqeen figured if it was worth mentioning, he should check it out. He went over to the other corner, and inside of a cage was the remnants of a woman that used to be.

Her hair was matted, and she stunk like garbage, or almost like a dead body.

"Hey, excuse me?"

The woman jumped when she heard Juaqeen's voice, and she went to the back of the cage.

Juaqeen looked in her eyes that were lit up by the moon, and his heart instantly broke. "Jayla?"

It was almost as if she was a lost woman, and in a way, she was.

There was no doubt in his mind that this was his Jayla, the mother of his child, and the love of his life.

He didn't know how he was going to get her out of this cage, and even if he did, he knew there was so much damage done, she was in an emotional and mental cage.

How did this happen? Everyone in his family and everything he touched seemed to crumble, but he made a promise to himself right then and there that no matter what, he would fix all of this shit.

Roman saw Juaqeen was lingering a little too long, so he came over to him and bent down.

"Who is this, son?"

Juaqeen shook his head and broke down into tears. He put his hands on the cage, and Jayla put on hers up as much as she could. Her arms were weak and skinny, her skin was hanging off of her body.

"I'ma save you, baby. I'ma save us all…"

J

uaqeen kicked the cage, repeatedly with all of his strength. After all of these years, he couldn't believe she was alive. He'd always hoped that somehow, she was, but he didn't know if it was possible or if it was all in his mind—something he'd made up. This was terrifyingly beautiful.

When the cage wouldn't open, Juaqeen snatched the gun away from his father and told Jayla to stand as far against the other side of the cage as she possibly could.

Jayla, who was discombobulated and completely surprised was so in shock, she didn't hear Juaqeen who was telling her to get back, but Juaqeen didn't have time for that. He had to get her out of there so that Lexxy could get to a hospital. Juaqeen fired the gun, startling Jayla out of whatever daze she was in.

The lock on the cage popped off, and the door opened. Jayla looked as though she wasn't used to personal interaction or any personal attention. The closer Juaqeen got to her, she cowered to the back of the cage, trying to scoot as far away as possible. Though she wanted to scream, her throat was so dry, she couldn't make a peep. Juaqeen reached into the cage and grabbed her gently, trying to help get her out of the cage. When he got a closer look, she was naked from the waist down. Juaqeen couldn't believe the love of his life had been treated so poorly, and he promised himself when the time came, he would kill whoever did this to her. Juaqeen removed his shirt and wrapped it around her waist.

"Come on, baby," Juaqeen whispered as he helped her stand to her feet. She was so skinny, skinnier than she had been when she was healthy. Jayla's two legs were entirely too wobbly, she couldn't stand up on her own. Like the hero he was, Juaqeen picked her up and held her like he had the last time he was with her.

Wild Bill and Lexxy were already in the car, waiting

for Roman and Juaqeen to join them. Wild Bill didn't want to start the car as not to bring attention to them until it was time. From the side of the house, Wild Bill could hear Cocaine tussling with who he assumed was Paul and Quentin, but if there was one thing they were all certain of: Cocaine could handle himself.

Roman and Juaqeen came stumbling out of the house with Jayla in Juaqeen's arms. Roman pulled the door open to the large blacked out SUV and helped Juaqeen lay her in the back seat, just in front of Lexxy who was laid out a row behind her.

Lexxy was in so much pain, she didn't have the energy to lean up and see what was going on. Her mind was on her baby and her husband. This entire time, she hadn't seen Cocaine, and she wondered where he was, but she was going in between consciousness and definitive unconsciousness, so she couldn't even ask if she wanted to what was happening.

Though Cocaine and Quentin were supposed to be having a fair fight, Cocaine was getting the best of him, so Paul had to jump in to rescue his brother. Several punches to the face, head, and ribs had left Quentin not only bloody but with broken and bruised ribs, not to mention the fact that Cocaine had kicked them in both of their chins, so they were sore all over and were having a problem regaining control over the fight, and that fact alone pissed Paul off. He was tasked with the same charge most older siblings are: protection, and he felt like he had failed to do so. It didn't help any that it had begun raining.

As sweat and rain mixed, clouding the three men's

vision, dripping down their faces, Paul grew tired of seeing his brother get his ass whooped, and there was only one thing he knew to do. Sure, Quentin had said he was going to play by the rules and fight like a man, but Paul never agreed to such bullshit.

Paul pulled his gun from his backside and pulled the hammer back, popping Cocaine right in the rib.

"Shit!" Cocaine yelled as he stumbled backwards.

Hearing the gunshot and with the car finally being loaded, Wild Bill was in the middle row, Juaqeen was in the front, Jayla and Lexxy in both of the back rows, and Roman driving, the SUV pulled up to the front of the house. Juaqeen hoped for Paul and Quentin's sake that one of them had been shot, but when they reached the front of the house, Juaqeen saw Cocaine on the ground, and he lost it. This day was already stressful enough. None of them had any rest, their minds were going haywire, and now, his emotions had been played on with Jayla, and his son was the icing on the cake.

Juaqeen jumped out of the passenger seat with the gun he'd snatched from Roman, pointing it at Paul as he moved to shield Cocaine from Paul possibly finishing the job. Juaqeen was prepared to shoot, but he was frozen by the words that were shouted in his direction.

"Don't! Don't shoot my son! Please, don't shoot!"

Those words were undeniable. There was no way Juaqeen could have mistaken them. He turned around, along with everyone else to face the shouting woman who was hanging out of the door.

"Wha—what did you just say?" Juaqeen asked as he

stared at her, wondering how something like this could be true.

"Those are my children, please…don—" Jayla couldn't finish her sentence. She fell out of the open door, and Juaqeen couldn't even move to save her from falling. Cocaine saw the woman who had fallen out and onto the ground, but there was no way she was who he thought she was. How in the hell could she be alive after all this time? Though Cocaine had been happy to see his father and was still a bit confused, this was something new. This was some shit that was unheard of. None of the people in his life knew how to stay dead, not that that was what he wanted, but he was used to them being gone. T, well he just wasn't used to.

Paul and Quentin were looking just as surprised. This woman, who had been in the basement of the abandoned home they'd overseen for years, was their mother? How could this be? This goes to show what happens when you do what your parents tell you to do without asking any questions. Sometimes loyalty can result in consequences unforeseen, like this.

If this was true, Cocaine, Quentin, and Paul were brothers, half-brothers, but brothers nonetheless.

Juaqeen finally snapped his mind back into reality. He helped Jayla back in the car and then ran out and got Cocaine who was holding his ribs that had completely gone numb.

Cocaine limped to the car with his father holding onto him. The trunk popped, and Cocaine climbed in the back, looking over the seat at Lexxy who was passed out. He moved the hair out of her beautiful face, taking a good look at her, and he promised he'd kill Paul and Quentin for doing this to her. She looked to be in pain, and the blood and wet spots between her legs let him know she was.

Before Cocaine lie down, he tried to process what happened, but there just wasn't enough time in the damn world to accept the fact that his grandfather, father, and his own mother were back in his life, and she was the mother of the two hellions who were trying to take him and his family out.

To Be Continued… the finale is up next!!!!

cocaine

lexxy

quentin

paul

dutch

wild bill

carley

cocaine & lexxy wedding

make it nastee

<u>Follow me on social mediaaaaaaa!</u>

tIKTOK: https://www.tiktok.com/@authornastee?_t=8oKW9zpRqcY&_r=1

FACEBOOK: https://www.tiktok.com/@authornastee?_t=8oKW9zpRqcY&_r=1

Facebook group: https://www.facebook.com/share/8XUtwdsL8SdE7EXN/

iNSTAGRAM:
https://www.instagram.com/makeitnastee_?igsh=
MWcwY3M5OHgxZDM0Mw%3D%3D&
utm_source=qr

acknowledgments